BTT 17
36a

July's People

ALSO BY NADINE GORDIMER

novels

A Guest of Honour `
The Late Bourgeois World
Occasion for Loving
A World of Strangers
The Lying Days
The Conservationist
Burger's Daughter

short stories

Livingstone's Companions
Not for Publication
Friday's Footprint
Six Feet of the Country
The Soft Voice of the Serpent
Selected Stories
A Soldier's Embrace

July's People

Nadine Gordimer

The Viking Press ◇ New York

Copyright © 1981 by Nadine Gordimer
All rights reserved
First published in 1981 by The Viking Press
625 Madison Avenue, New York, N.Y. 10022
Published simultaneously in Canada by
Penguin Books Canada Limited

Library of Congress Cataloging in Publication Data
Gordimer, Nadine.
July's people.
I. Title.
PR9369.3.G6J8   823   80-24877
ISBN 0-670-41048-9

Grateful acknowledgment is made to International Publishing Company
and Lawrence & Wishart, Ltd., for permission to reprint a quotation from
Selections from the Prison Notebooks of Antonio Gramsci, edited
and translated by Quintin Hoare and Geoffrey Nowell Smith.

Printed in the United States of America
Set in VIP Sabon

'The old is dying and the new cannot be born; in this interregnum there arises a great diversity of morbid symptoms.'

—Antonio Gramsci
Prison Notebooks

July's People

Y ou like to have some cup of tea?—
    July bent at the doorway and began that day for them
as his kind has always done for their kind.
    The knock on the door. Seven o'clock. In governors' resi-
dences, commercial hotel rooms, shift bosses' company bung-
alows, master bedrooms *en suite*—the tea-tray in black
hands smelling of Lifebuoy soap.
    The knock on the door
    no door, an aperture in thick mud walls, and the sack that
hung over it looped back for air, sometime during the short
night. *Bam, I'm stifling; her voice raising him from the dead,
he staggering up from his exhausted sleep.*
    No knock; but July, their servant, their host, bringing two
pink glass cups of tea and a small tin of condensed milk,
jaggedly-opened, specially for them, with a spoon in it.
    —No milk for me.—

—Or me, thanks.—

The black man looked over to the three sleeping children bedded-down on seats taken from the vehicle. He smiled confirmation: —They all right.—

—Yes, all right.— As he dipped out under the doorway: —Thank you, July, thank you very much.—

She had slept in round mud huts roofed in thatch like this before. In the Kruger Park, a child of the shift boss and his family on leave, an enamel basin and ewer among their supplies of orange squash and biscuits on the table coming clear as this morning light came. Rondavels adapted by Bam's ancestors on his Boer side from the huts of the blacks. They were a rusticism true to the continent; before air-conditioning, everyone praised the natural insulation of thatch against heat. Rondavels had concrete floors, thickly shined with red polish, veined with trails of coarse ants; in Botswana with Bam and his guns and hunter's supply of red wine. This one was the prototype from which all the others had come and to which all returned: below her, beneath the iron bed on whose rusty springs they had spread the vehicle's tarpaulin, a stamped mud and dung floor, above her, cobwebs stringy with dirt dangling from the rough wattle steeple that supported the frayed grey thatch. Stalks of light poked through. A rim of shady light where the mud walls did not meet the eaves; nests glued there, of a brighter-coloured mud—wasps, or bats. A thick lip of light round the doorway; a bald fowl entered with chicks cheeping, the faintest sound in the world. Its gentleness, ordinariness produced sudden, total disbelief. Maureen and Bam Smales. Bamford Smales, Smales, Caprano & Partners, Architects. Maureen Hetherington from Western Areas Gold Mines. Under 10s Silver Cup for Classical and Mime at the Johannesburg Eisteddfod. She closed her eyes again and the lurching motion of the vehicle swung in her head as the swell of the sea makes the land heave underfoot when the passenger steps ashore after a voyage. She fell asleep as, first sensorily dislocated by the assault of the vehicle's motion, then broken in and contained by its a-rhythm, she had slept from time to time in the three days and nights hidden on the floor of the vehicle.

People in delirium rise and sink, rise and sink, in and out of lucidity. The swaying, shuddering, thudding, flinging stops, and the furniture of life falls into place. The vehicle was the fever. Chattering metal and raving dance of loose bolts in the smell of the children's car-sick. She rose from it for gradually longer and longer intervals. At first what fell into place was what was vanished, the past. In the dimness and traced brightness of a tribal hut the equilibrium she regained was that of the room in the shift boss's house on mine property she had had to herself once her elder sister went to boarding-school. Picking them up one by one, she went over the objects of her collection on the bookshelf, the miniature brass coffee-pot and tray, the four bone elephants, one with a broken trunk, the khaki pottery bulldog with the Union Jack painted on his back. A lavender-bag trimmed with velvet forget-me-nots hung from the upright hinge of the adjustable mirror of the dressing-table, cut out against the window whose light was meshed by minute squares of the wire flyscreen, clogged with mine dust and dead gnats. The dented silver stopper of a cut-glass scent bottle was cemented to the glass neck by layers and years of dried Silvo polish. Her school shoes, cleaned by Our Jim (the shift boss's name was Jim, too, and so her mother talked of her husband as 'My Jim' and the house servant as 'Our Jim'), were outside the door. A rabbit with a brown patch like a birthmark over one eye and ear was waiting in his garden hutch to be fed... As if the vehicle had made a journey so far beyond the norm of a present it divided its passengers from that the master bedroom *en suite* had been lost, jolted out of chronology as the room where her returning consciousness properly belonged: the room that she had left four days ago.

The shapes of pigs passed the doorway and there were calls in one of the languages she had never understood. Once, she knew—she always knew—her husband was awake although still breathing stertorously as a drunk. She heard herself speak.

—Where is it?— She was seeing, feeling herself contained by the vehicle.

—He said hide it in the bush.—

Another time she heard something between a rustling and a gnawing. —What? What's that?—

He didn't answer. He had driven most of the time, for three days and three nights. If no longer asleep, stunned by the need of sleep.

She slowly began to inhabit the hut around her, empty except for the iron bed, the children asleep on the vehicle seats—the other objects of the place belonged to another category: nothing but a stiff rolled-up cowhide, a hoe on a nail, a small pile of rags and part of a broken Primus stove, left against the wall. The hen and chickens were moving there; but the slight sound she heard did not come from them. There would be mice and rats. Flies wandered the air and found the eyes and mouths of her children, probably still smelling of vomit, dirty, sleeping, safe.

The vehicle was a bakkie, a small truck with a three-litre engine, fourteen-inch wheels with heavy-duty ten-ply tyres, and a sturdy standard chassis on which the buyer fits a fibreglass canopy with windows, air-vents and foam-padded benches running along either side, behind the cab. It makes a cheap car-cum-caravan for white families, generally Afrikaners, and their half-brother coloureds who can't afford both. For more affluent white South Africans, it is a second, sporting vehicle for purposes to which a town car is not suited.

It was yellow. Bam Smales treated himself to it on his fortieth birthday, to use as a shooting-brake. He went trap-shooting to keep his eye in, out of season, and when winter came spent his weekends in the bush, within a radius of two hundred kilometres of his offices and home in the city, shooting guinea-fowl, red-legged partridge, wild duck and spur-wing geese. Before the children were born, he had taken his wife on hunting trips farther afield—to Botswana, and once, before the Portuguese régime was overthrown, to Moçambique. He would no sooner shoot a buck than a man; and he did not keep any revolver under his pillow to defend his wife, his children or his property in their suburban house.

The vehicle was bought for pleasure, as some women are said to be made for pleasure. His wife pulled the face of tasting something that set her teeth on edge, when he brought it home. But he defended the dyed-blonde jauntiness; yellow was cheerful, it repelled heat.

They stood round it indulgently, wife and family, the children excited, as it seemed nothing else could excite them, by a new possession. Nothing made them so happy as buying things; they had no interest in feeding rabbits. She had smiled at him the way she did when he spurted ahead of her and did what he wanted; a glimpse of the self that does not survive coupling. —Anything will spot you a mile off, in the bush.—

In various and different circumstances certain objects and individuals are going to turn out to be vital. The wager of survival cannot, by its nature, reveal which, in advance of events. How was one to know? Civil Emergency Planning Services will not provide. (In '76, after the Soweto Riots, pharmaceutical firms brought out a government-approved line in First Aid boxes.) The circumstances are incalculable in the manner in which they come about, even if apocalyptically or politically foreseen, and the identity of the vital individuals and objects is hidden by their humble or frivolous role in an habitual set of circumstances.

It began prosaically weirdly. The strikes of 1980 had dragged on, one inspired or brought about by solidarity with another until the walkout and the shut-down were lived with as contiguous and continuous phenomena rather than industrial chaos. While the government continued to compose concessions to the black trade unions exquisitely worded to conceal exactly concomitant restrictions, the black workers concerned went hungry, angry, and workless anyway, and the shop-floor was often all that was left of burned-out factories. For a long time, no one had really known what was happening outside the area to which his own eyes were witness. Riots, arson, occupation of the headquarters of international corporations, bombs in public buildings—the censorship of newspapers, radio and television left rumour and word-of-mouth as the only sources of information about this chronic state of uprising all over the country. At home, after weeks of rioting out of sight in Soweto, a march on Johannesburg of (variously estimated) fifteen thousand blacks had been stopped at the edge of the business centre at the cost of a (variously estimated) number of lives, black and white. The bank accountant for whom Bam had designed a house tipped off that if the situation in the city showed no signs of being contained (his phrase) the banks would have to declare a moratorium. So Bam, in a state of detached disbelief at his action, taking along a moulded plastic-foam box that had once held a Japanese hi-fi system, withdrew five thousand rands in notes and Maureen gave the requisite twenty-four hours' notice for withdrawal from her savings account and cleared it, one thousand seven hundred and fifty-six rands in notes which, secured by rubber bands, she carried home without incident in a woven grass shopping bag with Bam's suit from the dry cleaner folded ostentatiously on top.

And then the banks did not close. The blacks were held back (they were temporarily short of ammunition and they had long since given up the heroism of meeting bullets with sticks and stones) by the citizen force strengthened by white Rhodesian immigrants, some former Selous Scouts, accustomed to this sort of fighting, and the arrival of a plane-load of white mercenaries flown in from Bangui, Zaïre, Uganda— wherever it was they had been propping up the current Amins, Bokassas and Mobutus. The children stayed home from school but played wildly at street-fighting in the peaceful garden. The liquor store suddenly delivered wine and beer ordered weeks before, two black men in overalls embroidered with the legend of a brand of cane spirit carrying the cases into the kitchen and exchanging time-of-day jokingly with the servants. For the twentieth, the hundredth time, since the pass-burnings of the Fifties, since Sharpeville, since Soweto '76, since Elsie's River 1980, it seemed that all was quietening down again.

First the Smales had given the time left as ten years, then another five years, then as perhaps projected, shifted away into their children's time. They yearned for there to be no time left at all, while there still was. They sickened at the appalling thought that they might find they had lived out their whole lives as they were, born white pariah dogs in a black continent. They joined political parties and 'contact' groups in willingness to slough privilege it was supposed to be their white dog nature to guard with Mirages and tanks; they were not believed. They had thought of leaving, then, while they were young enough to cast off the blacks' rejection as well as white privilege, to make a life in another country. They had stayed; and told each other and everyone else that this and nowhere else was home, while knowing, as time left went by, the reason had become they couldn't get their money out—Bam's growing savings and investments, Maureen's little legacy of De Beers shares her maternal grandfather had left her, the house there was less and less opportunity of selling as city riots became a part of life. Once again, for the hundred-and-first time, thousands of blacks were imprisoned, broken glass was swept up, cut telephone lines were reconnected, radio and television assured that control was re-established. The husband and wife felt it was idiotic to have that money hidden in the house; they were about to put it back in the bank again...

When it all happened, there were the transformations of myth or religious parable. The bank accountant had been the legendary warning hornbill of African folk-tales, its flitting cries ignored at peril. The yellow bakkie that was bought for fun turned out to be the vehicle: that which bore them away from the gunned shopping malls and the blazing, unsold houses of a depressed market, from the burst mains washing round bodies in their Saturday-morning garb of safari suits, and the heat-guided missiles that struck Boeings carrying those trying to take off from Jan Smuts Airport. The cook-nanny, Nora, ran away. The decently-paid and contented male servant, living in their yard since they had married, clothed by them in two sets of uniforms, khaki pants for rough housework, white drill for waiting at table, given Wednesdays and alternate Sundays free, allowed to have his friends visit him and his town woman sleep with him in his room—he turned out to be the chosen one in whose hands their lives were to be held; frog prince, saviour, July.

He brought a zinc bath big enough for the children to sit in, one by one, and on his head, paraffin tins of water heated on one of the cooking-fires. She washed the children, then herself in their dirty water; for the first time in her life she found that she smelled bad between her legs, and—sending the children out and dropping the sack over the doorway—disgustedly scrubbed at the smooth lining of her vagina and the unseen knot of her anus in the scum and suds. Her husband took a chance and washed in the river—all these East-flowing rivers carried the risk of bilharzia infection.

July came back and forth with porridge, boiled wild spinach, and even a pawpaw, hard and green—the family's custom of finishing a meal with fruit ritualistically observed, somehow, by one so long habituated to them. No uniform here (he wore an illegibly faded T-shirt and dusty trousers, clothes he left to come back to on his two-yearly leave), but he went in and out the hut with the bearing he had had for fifteen years in their home; of service, not servile, understanding their needs and likings, allying himself discreetly with their standards and even the disciplining and indulgence of the children.

—We'll cook for ourselves, July. We must make our own fire.— The guest protesting at giving trouble; he and she caught the echo of those visitors who came to stay in her house and tipped him when they left.

He had brought wood for Bam, but was back again at dusk. He didn't trust them to look after themselves. —You want I make small fire now?— He was carrying a Golden Syrup tin full of milk. There was a little boy with him; earlier in the day he had chased curious black children away. —This my third-born, nearly same time like Victor. Victor he's twenty-one January, isn't it? This one he's Christmas Day.—

The white children had seen the servant's photograph of his children, in his wallet along with his pass-book, back there. They looked at the black child as at an impostor.

—Is from the goat, this milk we drink, I don't know if Gina she's going like it. Always Gina little bit fussy. Madam, you can boil it— He screwed up one eye and his mouth drew down the sides of his moustache, advising caution, most delicately acknowledging some lack of hygiene, if he were to compare the goat, the syrup tin, with the sterilized bottles from which he would take milk out of the refrigerator, back there.

The vehicle was moved from the bush, at night, to a group of abandoned huts within sight of but removed from those of

July's family. Bam did not use the headlights and was guided by July moving along in the dark ahead of him, as he had been for certain stretches of the journey. That way they had avoided both patrols and roving bands. July's knowledge or instinct that in country dorps the black petrol attendants often live in sheds behind the garage-and-general-store complex—on that they had kept going, on and on, although they had left with only enough fuel to take them less than half-way. He asked for notes from the plastic-foam box and, every time, came back with petrol, water, food. It was a miracle; it was all a miracle: and one ought to have known, from the sufferings of saints, that miracles are horror. How that load of human beings with the haphazard few possessions there was time to take along (the bag of oranges Maureen had run back to fetch from the kitchen, the radio Bam remembered so that they could hear what was happening behind them as they fled) could hope to arrive at the destination placed before them—that was an impossibility from minute to minute. —We can go to my home.— July said it, standing in the living-room where he had never sat down, as he would say 'We can buy little bit paraffin' when there was a stain to be removed from the floor. That he should have been the one to decide what they should do, that their helplessness, in their own house, should have made it clear to him that he must do this—the sheer unlikeliness was the logic of their position. There was nothing else to do but the impossible, now they had stayed too long. They put their children into the vehicle, covered them with a tarpaulin under which Maureen crawled, and drove. How the vehicle hadn't broken down, urged across the veld and mealie-fields, ground-nut fields, into dongas and through sluices whose stones were deep under the table of summer rains; how they had found their way, not daring to use the roads, taking three days and nights for a journey that could be done in a day's hard driving under normal conditions—but that was July, July knew the whole six hundred kilometres, had walked it, making a fire to keep the lions away at night where his path bordered and even passed through the Kruger Park, the first time he came to the city to look for work.

The vehicle was driven right within the encirclement of a roofless hut. Red as an anthill, thick clay walls had washed down to rejoin the earth here and there, and scrubby trees pushed through them like limbs of plumbing exposed in a half-demolished building. The vehicle flattened the tall weeds of the floor and a roof of foliage, thorn and parasitic creepers hid the yellow paint.

From the doorway of the hut they had been given she could make out the vehicle. Or thought she could; knew it was there. There was still a plastic demijohn of tap-water taken from the last dorp, hidden in it. She went secretly, observed from afar by whispering black children, to fetch rations for her children to drink. Within the hot metal that boomed hollowly where her weight buckled it, the vehicle was a deserted house re-entered. Trapped flies lay droning into unconsciousness on their backs. It was as if she had walked into that other abandoned house.

—You won't see it from the air.— They had watched two planes flying over, although at a great height. Bam was satisfied the vehicle would not draw a stray bomb shat by some aircraft from the black army's bases in Moçambique that might reconnoitre the bush and find a suspicious sign of white para-military presence in an area where even a broken-down car was a rarity.

July's home was not a village but a habitation of mud houses occupied only by members of his extended family. There was the risk that if, as he seemed to assume, he could reconcile them to the strange presence of whites in their midst and keep their mouths shut, he could not prevent other people, living scattered round about, who knew the look of every thorn-bush, from discovering there were thorn-bushes that overgrew a white man's car, and passing on that information to any black army patrol. If not acting upon it themselves?

July broke into snickering embarrassment at her ignorance of a kind of authority not understood—his; and anyway, he had told them—everybody—about the vehicle.

—Told them what?— She was confident of his wily good sense; he had worked for her for years. Often Bam couldn't follow his broken English, but he and she understood each other well.

—I tell them you give it to me.—

Bam blew laughter. —Who'll believe that.—

—They know, they know what it is happening, the trouble in town. The white people are chased away from their houses and we take. Everybody is like that, isn't it?—

—But you can't drive.— She was anxious, for their safety, he should be believed.

—How they know I'm not driving? Everybody is know I'm living fifteen years in town, I'm knowing plenty things.—

It was some days before the vehicle ceased to be the point of reference for their existence. What was left of the tinned food was still there; the box containing Victor's electric rac-ing-car track that it was discovered he must have put in under cover of adult confusion. There was nowhere, in this hut, to put anything: —It's not worthwhile dragging everything out.— But Victor nagged for his racing-car track. —It only means you'll have to dismantle it and pack it up again.—

He had the habit of standing in front of her with his de-mands; she walked round him.

He planted himself again. —When are we going?—

—Vic, where's there to set it up? And there's no electricity, you can't run it.—

—I want to show it.—

—To whom?—

The black children who watched the hut from afar and scuttled, as if her glance were a stone thrown among them, re-formed a little way off.

—But tell them they mustn't touch it. I don't want my things messed up and broken. You must tell them.—

She laughed as adults did, in the power they refuse to use. —I tell them? They don't understand our language.—

The boy said nothing but kicked steadily at the dented, rusted bath used for their ablutions.

—Don't. D'you hear me? That's July's.—

The demijohn of water was empty. Royce, the littlest, kept asking for Coca-Cola: —Then *buy* some. Go to the shop-man and *buy* some.— She put paraffin tins of river water on the fire. She would cool the boiled water overnight; —It's madness to let them drink that stuff straight from the river. They'll get ill.—

Bam got the blaze going. —I assure you, they've been drinking water wherever they find it, already...it's impossible to stop them.—

—What're we going to do if they get ill?—

But he didn't answer and she didn't expect him to. There lay between them and all such questions the unanswerable: they were lucky to be alive.

The seats from the vehicle no longer belonged to it; they had become the furniture of the hut. Outside in an afternoon cooled by a rippled covering of grey luminous clouds, she sat on the ground as others did. Over the valley beyond the kraal of euphorbia and dead thorn where the goats were kept: she knew the vehicle was there. A ship that had docked in a far country. Anchored in the khakiweed, it would rust and be stripped to hulk, unless it made the journey back, soon.

A dresser made of box-wood in imitation of the kind whose prototype might have been seen in a farmer's kitchen had shelf-edgings of fancy-cut newspaper and held the remainder of the set of pink glass cups and saucers.

July presented her to his wife. A small, black-black, closed face, and huge hams on which the woman rested on the earth floor as among cushions, turning this way and that as she took a tin kettle from the wisp of hearth ashes to pour tea, silently, over the mug an old lady held, and adjusted the feeding-bottle in the hands of a child past the age of weaning whose eyes were turning up in sleep on her own lap. She frowned appealingly under July's chivvying voice, swayed, murmured greeting sounds.

—She say, she can be very pleased you are in her house. She can be very glad to see you, long time now, July's people—

But she had said nothing. Maureen took her hand and then that of the old lady, who was somebody's mother—July's or his wife's. The old lady wore gilt drop ear-rings and a tin brooch with red glass stones pinned her black snail-shell turban. Thin bare feet soled with ash stuck out from the layers of skirt in which she squatted. She demanded something of July, growling a clearing of the throat before each question and looking, her head cocked up, at the white woman who smiled and inclined herself in repeated greeting. There were several others, young women and half-grown girls, in the hut. His sister, wife's sister-in-law, one of his daughters; he introduced them with a collective sweep in terms of kinship and not by name. The small child was his last-born, conceived, as all his children were, on one of his home-leaves and born in his absence. Maureen provided presents for him to send home on her behalf, at the news of each birth. And to this woman, July's wife, never seen, never imagined, had sent toys for the children and whatever it seemed surely any woman, no matter where or how she lived, could use: a night-gown, a handbag. When July returned from leave he would bring back with him in return a woven basket as a gift from his unknown wife, his home—in one of these baskets she had carried the money from the bank. His town woman was a respectable office cleaner who wore crimplene two-piece dresses on her days off. She ironed his clothes with Maureen's iron and chatted to Maureen when they met in the yard. The subject was usually a son being put through high school in Soweto on his mother's earnings; it was understood July's responsibility was to his own family, far away. The town woman had no children fathered by her lover; once had put a hand under her breasts with the gesture with which women declare themselves in conscious control of their female destiny: —It's all finished—I'm sterilized at the clinic.— In confidence: her black, city English sophisticated in the vocabulary relevant to the kind of life led there.

It was early morning but in their hut the women were dreamy, as at the end of the day; a furzy plank of sunlight rested from a single pane-sized aperture in the walls across the profile of a young girl, the twitching, hump-knuckles of the old lady, the fat spread legs of the sated child. On an iron bedstead tidily made up with fringed plaid blankets one of the half-grown girls was plaiting the hair on the bent head of another. Perhaps they had been out since first light gathering wood or working in their fields—Maureen was aware, among them in the hut, of not knowing where she was, in time, in the order of a day as she had always known it.

Why do they come here? Why to us?—
His wife had accepted his dictum, when he arrived that night in a white man's bakkie with a visitation of five white faces floating in the dark. Given up the second bed, borrowed a Primus for them; watched him, in the morning, take the beautiful cups he had once brought her from the place of his other life. His mother had given up her hut—the trees for the walls and roof-poles felled and raised by him, the mud of the walls mixed and built up by his mother and herself, that was due to have a new roof next thatching season. Both women had moved about under his bidding without argument. But that was not the end of it. He knew that would not be the end of it.

—You don't understand. Nowhere else to go. I've told you.—

His wife jerked her chin in exaggerated parody of accord.

She hung her head to her hunched shoulder as she had done as a girl. —White people here! Didn't you tell us many times how they live, there. A room to sleep in, another room to eat in, another room to sit in, a room with books (she had a Bible), I don't know how many times you told me, a room with how many books... Hundreds I think. And hot water that is made like the lights we see in the street at Vosloos-dorp. All these things I've never seen, my children have never seen—the room for bathing—and even you, there in the yard you had a room for yourself for bathing, and you didn't even wash your clothes in there, there was a machine in some other room for that— Now you tell me *nowhere*.—

She had her audience. The young girls who were always in her hut with her tittered.

—They had to get out, they had to go. People are burning those houses. Those big houses! You can't imagine those houses. The whites are being killed in their houses. I've seen it—the whole thing just blow up, walls, roof.—

His wife rubbed a forefinger up and down behind her ear. —He has a gun. The children saw there's a gun, he keeps it in the roof.—

—When they come, one gun is no use. If he could chase them away one day they would come back the next. There's trouble! Unless you've been there, you can't understand how it is.—

His mother's hands were never still. The four finger-tips of each beat ceaselessly at the ball of the thumb—the throb of an old heart exposed there, like the still-beating heart in the slit chest of a creature already dead. —White people must have their own people somewhere. Aren't they living every-where in this world? Germiston, Cape Town—you've been to many places, my son. Don't they go anywhere they want to go? They've got money.—

—Everywhere is the same. They are chasing the whites out.

The whites are fighting them. All those towns are the same. Where could he run with his family? His friends are also running. If he tried to go to a friend in another town, the friend wouldn't be there. It's true he can go where he likes. But when he gets there, he may be killed.—

They listened; with them, no one could tell if they were convinced.

—You used to write and say how you were looking after the house by yourself—feeding their dog, their cat. That time when you were even sleeping inside the house, thieves came and broke the window where you were sleeping—I don't know, one of those rooms they have... He went away, *overseas*, didn't he.—

The English word broke the cadence of their language. *Overseas*. The concept was as unfamiliar to his wife as the shaping of the word by her tongue, but he had carried the bags of departure, received postcards of skyscrapers and snow-covered mountains, answered telephone calls from countries where the time of day was different.

—You know about the big airport where the planes fly *overseas*? It wasn't working. And before that they shot down a plane with white people who were running away.—

—Who shot? Black people? Our people? How could they do that.— The old woman was impatient with him. —I've seen those planes, they pass over high in the sky, you even see them go behind clouds. You can hear them after you can't see them any more.—

—Over in Moçambique, our people have got some special kind of guns or bombs. They travel very far and very high. They've even got those things in Daveyton and KwaThema and Soweto now—right near town. They hit the plane and it burst in the air. Everyone was burned to death.—

His mother made the stylized, gobbling exclamations that both ward off disaster and attribute it to fate. —What will the white people do to us now, God must save us.—

◇ 20

Her son, who had seen the white woman and the three children cowered on the floor of their vehicle, led the white face behind the wheel in his footsteps, his way the only one in a wilderness, was suddenly aware of something he had not known. —They can't do anything. Nothing to us any more.—

—White people. They are very powerful, my son. They are very clever. You will never come to the end of the things they can do.—

When he was in the company of the women it was like being in the chief's court, where the elders sitting in judgment wander in and out and the discussion of evidence is taken up, now where they drift outside to take a breath of air or relieve themselves among their tethered horses and bicycles hitched against trees, now back in the court-room at whatever point the proceedings have moved on to. His mother went out to pluck a chicken whose neck he'd just wrung. His wife asked the young girls whether they thought she was going to do without water all day? How much longer were they going to hang about with their mouths open? One of the girls was bold but respectful: —*Tatani*, I want to ask, is it true you also had a room for bathing, like the one they had?—

—Oh yes, bath, white china lavatory, everything.—

They could only laugh, how could they visualize his quarters, not so big as the double garage adjoining, with in his room the nice square of worn carpet that was once in the master bedroom.

—There are eggs in the belly—it would still have given us eggs! You should have taken the white one with the broken foot, I told you.— The old woman was shouting from beyond the doorway.

—What is it she wants?—

—You killed the wrong fowl... But I don't know what it's all about.—

He called back. —Exactly. *Mhani*, that one with the bad

foot is a young one. It will lay well next year, even.—

The white woman's hand, when she stood there and offered it—the first time, touching white skin. His wife went with her mother-in-law sometimes to the dorp to hawk green mealies or the brooms the old lady made, outside the Indian store; it had happened that a white from the police post had bought from her sack of cobs, and cents had dropped from the white hand to hers. But she had never actually touched that skin before.

She fell again into the mannerism of holding her head to one side that had been bashful and that he had found so attractive, inviting him and escaping him, when she was a young girl, and that had become, in the years he was away in the city, something different, a gesture repelling, withdrawing, evasive and self-absorbed. —The face—I don't know... not a nice, pretty face. I always thought they had beautiful dresses. And the hair, it's so funny and ugly. What do they do to make it like that, dark bits and light bits. Like the tail of a dirty sheep. No. I didn't think she'd be like that, a rich white woman.—

—They looked different there—you should have seen the clothes in their cupboard. And the glasses—for visitors, when they drink wine. Here they haven't got anything—just like us.—

She sharply reproached the baby who, staggering around on legs braced wide for balance, had picked up fowl droppings and successfully conveyed the mess to its mouth. Her forefinger hooked unthinkingly round the soft membranes, awareness of the small body was still as part of her own. The man was excluded. She flicked the chalky paste off her fingers. —There'll be no more money coming every month.—

Without his white people back there, without the big house where he worked for them, she would not be getting those letters (yes, she had been to school, he would not have married a woman who could not read their own language) that came from his other life, his other self, and provided for those who could not follow him there. Not even in dreams; not even now, when she had seen his white people.

Bam could help July mend such farming tools—scarcely to be called equipment—as he and his villagers owned. The span of yokes and traces they shared, taking turns to plough, was kept in a special hut where no one lived. The heavy chains trailed across the floor. Hoes hung from the roof. There was the musty, nutty smell of stored grain in baskets. Someone had been there, picking over beans on one of the mats used as table-tops or bowls: Maureen saw the arrangement as broken beads set aside from good ones, choices made by someone momentarily absent—the dioramas of primitive civilizations in a natural history museum contrive to produce tableaux like that.

Bam was determined to rig up a water-tank, the round, corrugated tin kind, that had somehow been lugged that far into the bush but never installed. July laughed, and gave it a kick (as Victor had the bath).

—No, I mean it. If we can get hold of a bag of cement, we can make a foundation. I saw some old piping lying somewhere...? You could have quite a decent rain-water supply all through the rainy months. It's a waste. The women won't need to go to the river. It'll be much better to drink than river water.—

There was no bag of cement; but they worked together more or less as they did when Bam expected July to help him with the occasional building or repair jobs that had to be done to maintain a seven-roomed house and swimming-pool. Bam made do with stones for a foundation. He kept the radio near and at the hours when news bulletins were read she would appear from wherever she might be. They stood and listened together. There were other radios in the community, bellowing, chattering, twanging pop music, the sprightly patter of commercials in a black language; the news reader's gardening-talk voice spoke English only to the white pair, only for them. They didn't comment and each watched the other's face. But whatever each hoped to find there, of a sudden new decision made, or dreaded to find, of new grounds for fear, did not appear. There was fierce fighting round Jan Smuts Airport; the city centre, under martial law, had been quiet last night, but mortar fire was heard and confused reports had been received of heavy fighting in the eastern and northern suburbs. The Red Cross appealed for blood. The gasworks had been attacked and the explosion had started a fire that spread to suburban houses; Bam's eyebrows flew up and exposed his gaze—only across the valley, the freeway, from the house they had chosen to build in a quiet suburb. U.S. Congress was debating the organization of a United States government airlift for American nationals. It was not known from where it would operate; Cape Town, Durban and Port Elizabeth airports were closed, and their ports bombed and blockaded. Maureen looked away where a young boy was emptying a basket head-load of stones as July directed; she had been for trying to get to the coast.

Lucky to be alive. Neither could expect the other to say what would come next; what to do next; not yet. He arranged the stones brought from some other attempt to build something that had fallen into ruin. That was how people lived, here, rearranging their meagre resources around the bases of nature, letting the walls of mud sink back to mud and then using that mud for new walls, in another clearing, among other convenient rocks. No one remembered where the water-tank came from. July said he would ask the old woman but never did, although she sat outside the women's hut most of the day, on the ground, making brooms out of some special grasses the women collected. The water-tank was from back there, like the Smales and their children; the white man was the one to make a place for it here.

Beyond the clearing—the settlement of huts, livestock kraals, and the stumped and burned-off patches which were the lands—the buttock-fold in the trees indicated the river and that was the end of measured distance. Like clouds, the savannah bush formed and re-formed under the changes of light, moved or gave the impression of being moved past by the travelling eye; silent and ashy green as mould spread and always spreading, rolling out under the sky before her. There were hundreds of tracks used since ancient migrations (never ended; her family's was the latest), not seen. There were people, wavering circles of habitation marked by euphorbia and brush hedges, like this one, fungoid fairy rings on grass—not seen. There were cattle cracking through the undergrowth, and the stillness of wild animals—all not to be seen. Space; so confining in its immensity her children did not know it was there. Royce headed a delegation: —Can't we go to a film today? Or tomorrow?— (The postponement an inkling, the confusion of time with that other dimension, proper to this place.) Even though Gina and Victor were old enough to know cinemas had been left behind, they did not stop him asking, and sulked and quarrelled afterwards on the car-seat beds in the hut, scratching flea-bites. Maureen could not walk out into the boundlessness. Not so far as to take the dog around the block or to the box to post a letter. She could go to the river but no farther, and not often. When she did go she did so believing it better not to go at all than risk being seen, now.

July came to fetch her family's clothes for the women to wash down there.

—I can do it myself.— They had so few, they wore so little; the children had abandoned shoes, there was no question of a fresh pair of shorts and socks every day.

But he stood in the manner of one who will not go away without what he has come for. —Then I must carry water for you, make it hot, everything.—

She saw she could not expect to be indulged, here, in any ideas he knew nothing about.

—Will your wife do it? I must pay.—

It was women's business, in his home. His short laugh tugged tight with his fingers at the ends of the loose bundle she had made. —I don't know who or who. But you can pay.—

—And soap?— She was cherishing a big cake of toilet soap, carefully drying it after each use and keeping it on top of the hut wall, out of reach of the children.

—I bring soap.—

Soap he had remembered to take from her store-cupboard? His clean clothes smelled of Lifebuoy she bought for them— the servants. He didn't say; perhaps merely not to boast his foresight. She was going to ask—and quite saw she could not.

—I'll pay for it.— Bundles of notes were bits of paper, in this place; did not represent, to her, the refrigerator full of frozen meat and ice-cubes, the newspapers, water-borne sewage, bedside lamps money could not provide here. But its meaning was not dissociated, for July's villagers. She saw how when she or Bam, who were completely dependent on these people, had nothing but bits of paper to give them, not even clothes—so prized by the poor—to spare, they secreted the paper money in tied rags and strange crumpled pouches about their persons. They were able to make the connection between the abstract and the concrete. July—and others like him, all the able men went away to work—had been sending these bits of paper for so long and had been bringing, over fifteen years (that meant seven home-leaves), many things that bits of paper could be transformed into, from the bicycle Bam had got for him at a discount to the supermarket pink glass teacups.

July's wife's hut, his own hut, the huts of three or four other families within the family, their goat-kraal, the chicken-coops made of twiggy dead branches staved into the earth in a rough criss-cross of hoops, the pig-pen enclosed by the fusion of organic and inorganic barriers—thorny aloes, battered hub-caps salvaged from wrecked cars, plates of crumbling tin, mud bricks; the hut where the farming implements were kept—these were the objectives and daily landmarks available. She moved between them neither working as others did nor able to do nothing as others did. She did have one book—a thick paperback snatched up in passing, until that moment something bought years ago and never read, perhaps it was meant for this kind of situation: Manzoni's *I Promessi Sposi*, in translation as *The Betrothed*. She did not want to begin it because what would happen when she had read it? There was no other. Then she overcame the taboo (if she did not read, they would find a solution soon; if she did read the book, they would still be here when it was finished). She dragged the lame stool July had supplied 'for the children' out where she had a view of the bush and began. But the transport of a novel, the false awareness of being within another time, place and life that was the pleasure of reading, for her, was not possible. She *was* in another time, place, consciousness; it pressed in upon her and filled her as someone's breath fills a balloon's shape. She was already not what she was. No fiction could compete with what she was finding she did not know, could not have imagined or discovered through imagination.

They had nothing.

In their houses, there was nothing. At first. You had to stay in the dark of the hut a long while to make out what was on the walls. In the wife's hut a wavy pattern of broad white and ochre bands. In others—she did not know whether or not she was welcome where they dipped in and out all day from dark to light like swallows—she caught a glimpse of a single painted circle, an eye or target, as she saw it. In one dwelling where she was invited to enter there was the tail of an animal and a rodent skull, dried gut, dangling from the thatch. Commonly there were very small mirrors snapping at the stray beams of light like hungry fish rising. They reflected nothing. An impression—sensation—of seeing something intricately banal, manufactured, replicated, made her turn as if someone had spoken to her from back there. It was in the hut where the yokes and traces for the plough-oxen were. She went inside again and discovered insignia, like war medals, nailed just to the left of the dark doorway. The enamel emblem's red cross was foxed and pitted with damp, bonded with dirt to the mud and dung plaster that was slowly incorporating it. The engraved lettering on the brass arm-plaque had filled with rust. The one was a medallion of the kind presented to black miners who pass a First Aid exam on how to treat injuries likely to occur underground, the other was a black miner's badge of rank, the highest open to him. Someone from the mines; someone had gone to the gold mines and come home with these trophies. Or they had been sent home; and where was the owner? No one lived in this hut. But someone had; had had possessions, his treasures displayed. Had gone away, or died—was forgotten or was commemorated by the evidence of these objects left, or placed, in the hut. Mine workers had been coming from out of these places for a long, long time, almost as long as the mines had existed. She read the brass arm-plaque: BOSS BOY.

The shift boss's gang earn recognition and advancement. He is proud of his BOSS BOY; some among the succession of incumbents have been recruited again and again from the kraals, the huts, repeating the migrant worker's nine- or eighteen-month contract for the whole period of My Jim's own working life; on Western Areas, while his girls are growing up ambitious to be ballet dancers.

A white schoolgirl is coming across the intersection where the shops are, chewing gum and moving to the tune of summer-afternoon humming. In step beside her is a woman of the age blacks retain between youth and the time when their sturdy and comfortable breasts and backsides become leaden weight, their good thick legs slow to a stop—old age. The black woman chews gum, too; her woollen cap is over one ear and she carries on her head a school case amateurishly stencilled in blue, MAUREEN HETHERINGTON. When the black woman makes to move against the traffic light suddenly gone red, the white girl grabs her hand to stop her, and they continue to hold hands, loosely and easily, while waiting for the light to change. Then they caper across together. Lydia scarcely needs to put up the other hand to steady the heavy case; she does so as one jaunties the set of a hat.

The pair are to be seen going like this, over the intersection at the local shops and the short-cut through the open veld (later there was an industrial area established there, the metal box factory and the potato crisps plant) to the mine married quarters. The shift bosses' houses are behind the recreation centre where ballet classes are held. Lydia has the back-door key of the house—shift boss My Jim's wife works in an estate agent's office and is out all day. Our Jim cleans the shoes and digs in the garden. Lydia has her time to herself, her housework is varied by frequent saunters to the shops where she goes to pick up a loaf, starch for the washing, or simply to meet and talk to other black people on similar errands. Maureen often bumps into her there, on her way home from school. Lydia expects her; maybe she sets out to do some shopping at the time she knows Maureen will be coming off the school bus. Once met, they are in no hurry; it is a hot time of day. Lydia sits on Maureen's case, continuing the long conversations she was engaged in before the girl was sighted, and Maureen goes into the Greek shop to get a Coke, which they share, mouth-about, and—if she has the cash—some gum or chocolate. Lydia swings the case—it contains a blazer, gym shoes as well as a load of books—onto her head. Sometimes they giggle and are in cahoots —Don't tell you saw, hey Lydia—(When she has come from school on the back of a boy's bicycle instead of safely by bus.) —Darling, how can I tell? You are my true friend, isn't it?— At other times Lydia is in a chastising, critical mood. It is directed first at 'those people': anyone with whom she has been wrangling over Fah-Fee bets or the complicated ethics of the 'club' to which she belongs, into whose funds each member pays part of her wages every month so that each in turn may have a bonus month when she is the recipient of the sum of all the others' contributions. —That woman! The sister-in-law of Gladys, she's holding the money, but I'm telling her, why if you holding you not paying in like everybody? Why you must get your month, but I'm short— Then the mood is turned on the girl, brooding over buried misdemeanours. —Maureen, you know your father he's getting cross if you going lose that thing again like last time— (The battery lantern, from the camping kit in his garage workshop; she promised it as a spotlight for the school nativity play.) —Maureen, why you take the pillows from your bed, let your friends make them dirty on the grass? Then your mother she's going shout me when she sees those marks in the washing, the dog with his feet and everything—

—Lovey, don't worry. I'll tell ma the dog came in and jumped on my bed. I'll put everything back, I promise you— Hanging wheedlingly round her neck, that was lighter than the rest of her (but how was she, naked; she was very prudish about the body and the functions of the body, had never revealed herself in a stage of undress further than her nylon bloomers and bare, lifted underarms, dingy purplish). The neck smelled of clean ironing, fish-frying, and the whiffs that came up from her feet that walked and sweated in plastic-soled slippers. The plump neck had three 'strings of pearls', the graceful lines of a young woman; she must have been only in her late twenties or early thirties.

One afternoon a photographer took a picture of Maureen and Lydia. They saw him dancing about on bent legs to get them in focus, just there at the shops while they crossed the road. When he had taken his photographs he came up and asked them if they minded. Lydia was in command; she put her hands on her hips, without disturbing the balance of the burden on her head. —But you must send us a picture. We like to have the picture.— He promised, and aimed at them again as they went on their way. He had not written down the address, Number 20, Married Quarters, Western Areas Gold Mines, so how could they get the photograph? Years later someone showed it to Maureen Smales in a *Life* coffee-table book about the country and its policies. White *herren-volk* attitudes and life-styles; the marvellous photograph of the white schoolgirl and the black woman with the girl's school case on her head.

Why had Lydia carried her case?

Did the photographer know what he saw, when they crossed the road like that, together? Did the book, placing the pair in its context, give the reason she and Lydia, in their affection and ignorance, didn't know?

At least for Bam the days were roughly divided into categories of work and rest. The third category, that organized suburban invention called leisure, did not exist, except as the talking and beer-drinking that began on Saturday morning and died down into sleep and revived again, until late in the course of Sunday night. There was some sort of hymn-singing that rose out of the beery kind, some kind of circling with little flags like the green-and-white flags carried by the Zionist Church zealots to their services on vacant lots in the city—maybe a Sunday church gathering mixed up with the spontaneity of drink that sent men and women slowly dancing, each on his own turntable of dust. Maureen could recognize July's quick voice and baritone laughter, holding the floor among country people. On their second Saturday Bam was offered and took beer with them; July intervened with a mug for him, while others drank from a clay pot, swilling over, passed round. Bam stayed as long as was polite—the men pressed drink upon him and approved, kindly teasing with leering, pretended admiration, when he seemed to relish their liquor. July strode about declaiming proprietarily an anecdote that obviously referred to this man who had been his employer, the guest and stranger.

Bam came back to the hut with something of the appropriate, slightly foolish expression of good-natured participation on his face; he hadn't understood a word. The maize brew was soporific; there was the constant subliminal feeling between him and her that they must discuss, *talk*. How to get out of here? Where to? But he was either putting up the water-tank, or the children—the children were generally around, as the blacks' children were always about their adults. And now he was sleepy, although for the moment the children were out of the way, fascinated by two oil-drums covered with cowhide that were being banged by dedicated young men who did not tire, only went into a lull now and then, a sleeper's breathing changing with his level of consciousness—the soft, lazy thud from a single drum-stick keeping the rhythm unbroken until it was quickened and orchestrated again.

—I caught Royce wiping his behind with a stone, this morning.—

Bam lay spread on the iron bed neither had room to turn on, shared at night. He didn't open his eyes but his naked diaphragm sucked in with amusement, and creaked the bed. —Well, a good thing he's acquired the technique. How long d'you think your toilet rolls will last?—

It was true that it was difficult to get the children to remember to bury the paper along with the turd; it was disgusting to find shit-smeared scraps blowing about—and being relished by the pigs, as she saw. She would have thought toilet rolls were some of the few essentials she had thought to bring. The things that had got in, bundled along (let alone the racing-car track Victor had smuggled)! She came upon a gadget for taking the dry cleaner's tags off clothes without breaking your nails. There were other gadgets, noticed in use about the settlement, she privately recognized as belonging to her: a small knife-grinder that had been in the mine house kitchen before her own, a pair of scissors in the form of a stork with blades for beak that she actually saw in July's hand when he reproached the old woman for trimming his baby's toenails with a razor blade. These things were once hers, back there; he must have filched them long ago. What else, over the years? Yet he was perfectly honest. When he was cleaning the floor, and found a cent rolled there, he would put it on Bam's bedside table. They had never locked anything, not even their liquor cupboard. If she had not happened—by what chance in a million, by what slow certain grind between the past and its retribution—to be here now, she would never have missed these things: so honesty is how much you know about anybody, that's all.

The terse habits engendered by the tension of the journey stayed with the couple. They communicated mainly about decisions neither wanted to take responsibility for without the other. Bam did not regard the malaria prophylactics she had not forgotten as he did her pack of blue toilet rolls. —Should we be saving them for the children?—

She doled out his pill and took hers, dry, swallowing repeatedly to get the galling bitterness down. —If we died of malaria, what would happen to them.—

There were many silences between them, when each waited for the other to say what might have to be said.

He was wearily, boredly trusting. —They would look after them. *He'd* look after them. Until someone came.—

—Who comes?—

—'The Cubans'.—

They began to banter and laugh. They had always—from a distance—admired Castro, the bourgeois white who succeeded in turning revolutionary.

—The Russians...—

—How many packets have we got left?—

—Six, I think.—

—Good god. Such a lot of pills!— His voice became low, murmuring, elliptical. This was the form of intimacy that had taken the place of love-talk between them. —Mmh?...did you expect we'd be staying a long time?—

—Well, will we?—

The radio station they depended on had been off the air for twenty-four hours; must have been a battle going on for control of the station. Broadcasts had been resumed again without comment. If the blacks had succeeded, there would have been the burst of martial music, the triumphant announcement, a new name for the country. But there were only reports of an RPG7 rocket-propelled grenade attack on the Carlton Centre, followed by occupation of the five-star hotel there by black forces.

She went down on her hunkers, resting her backside on one of the car seats. There was no nail-file; often she sat examining her broken nails, taking the rind of dirt from under them, as she did now, with a piece of fine wire, a thorn, whatever presented itself in the dust around her. —I used to think, one day I'd like to see where he lived, to make the trip home with him. I knew it would never come off.—

—No...the sort of thing that sounds fun...it was pretty impossible, then.—

—In that way.— In her pause, he said nothing. —You know. Combining it with a shooting trip for you. In the children's holidays. Bringing all the camping stuff. The portable fridge. What'd I imagine?—

He wriggled to show he was composing himself for a nap.

—Walking in here with presents for them, all lined up clapping their hands together in greeting. Telling the kids, this is *his* home, this is how he lives, see how cleverly July builds houses for himself. Telling everybody at home we actually drove him all the way to the bundu, visited him as a friend.—

Bam suddenly remembered, touching the rill of sleep, how they had run in haste and confusion. The malaria pills: —Where'd you get such a supply? Surely we didn't have them in the bathroom cupboard?—

—I looted. From the pharmacy. After they attacked the shops.—

The last thing he saw before he fell asleep was her face closed to him in the unconscious, matriarchal frown of necessity performed without question, without reasoning; the same frown she had had turned up to her by July's wife, in the women's hut—if he had been there to see it. He woke to hear the engine of the vehicle revving. —Maureen, what do you think you're *doing*!— He swayed in shock, sitting upright on the bed.

But she was in the hut with him. He shouted at her. —Who's playing around? That bloody little Victor! You gave him the keys?—

—I? I haven't any key.— On a precarious ledge of existence; no room to attack one another. Like the bed. They trembled, tottered, the dimness of the hut broke back and forth against, between them. She ran out.

She ran to where she knew the vehicle was, always, even when she wasn't looking. It was being driven off, jerkily but with growing confidence and speed as it cleared the deserted ruin and rocked onto a cattle path. She saw the backs of two black heads, driver and passenger. As she came back into the hut, he remembered, told her, told himself: —July's got the keys. He wanted to lock up something in there. Parts for his bicycle. His wife lets other people walk off with them.—

—Someone else's driving.—

—But it's him.—

—I couldn't see. Just the heads.—

Bam got up and had the menacing aspect of maleness a man has before the superego has gained control of his body, come out of sleep. His penis was swollen under his rumpled trousers. He went off round the huts, from one to another. A few men were sleeping in preparation for going back to the beer-drink. None of the women he encountered could speak his languages. The drums were in his head insistently. His sons had tired of watching the tireless drummers and were playing with skeletal carts, home-made of twisted wire by the black children, they had exchanged for the model cars from Victor's racing track. The cars had been broken up, the segments kept as objects in themselves by those who had so few that useless possession itself was the treasure. His daughter was eating mealie-meal with her fingers, from a pot shared with two or three other small girls. She called to claim him boastfully before them. —Hey, daddy!— In the group of drinkers he made himself understood; they asked one another questions, argued, and one who could speak a few words not of English but of Afrikaans said July 'had gone'. Somewhere. With someone. Another added, in English —He did not tell me. We do not know.—

Thought he made himself understood; couldn't ask them what he was thinking, what he really needed to have denied by them because it was so extraordinary, couldn't ever happen—like the fact of Bam and Maureen Smales and those three white children, here in this place. One can draw supposition and dread only from what one comes to know, over the years. In Rhodesia, during the war, it was said guerrillas had forced people at torture-point to co-operate with them. The white Selous Scouts had done the same. He couldn't get an answer out of anyone: had July perhaps been picked up by a passing patrol, or informed on and taken away to be questioned, forced with a gun at his ear to give up the white man's vehicle?

The facts that contradicted this did not bring the reassurance they should have. If this was what had happened, why hadn't there been a search of the settlement? Why did people go on drinking beer and joking—that was what all the shouts seemed to be about, just laughter and the quarrelsome, obsessive stories of people getting drunk.

There was nowhere to run to. Nothing to get away in. All he could say to Maureen was that it was July. July.

—He's not around.—

—When did he get the keys?—

—Oh, the other day.—

There was nothing to be remarked or reproached, in that, between them. *He* had been in charge on the journey, they were on his ground, here. He knew what was best. —It wasn't only his stuff. He says we ought to keep the vehicle locked because of the tools, too.— July apparently knew his relatives; when the vehicle's tools had been used to mend the old harrow, there were people who expected to borrow them but July didn't trust that they would be returned.

She knew only where to place her feet, precariously on the solid ground of footholds. She had steadied from the position where she almost had been knocked off balance. She sat on a car seat picking burrs from a child's jersey and making them into a careful pile so no bare foot would be hurt, accidentally treading on one.

When July was not about—only the two of them. He felt humbled, towards Maureen, but saw she did not share this— she was frightened into sulks?

But she got up and gathered the burrs and went to throw

them in the embers of their cooking-fire outside, making sure, with a strange precision, that they took the flame properly. She was someone handling her being like an electrical appliance she has discovered can fling one apart at a wrong touch. Not fear, but knowledge that the shock, the drop beneath the feet, happens to the self alone, and can be avoided only alone.

He wanted to call the children into the hut but did not know how to explain the necessity he felt, or if she shared it. If she said 'Why?', what would he say? He had a gun; he had brought his twelve-bore shot-gun as she had remembered toilet paper. It was hidden thrust up into the thatch, there above their heads as they stood in this hut where there was no room to hide anything from one another. What place was there for a white man's gun among these people who had taken them in without asking why they should expect to be sheltered, fed, hidden?

If he took it out and killed, could that be a defence against what might come, once outside July's protection? I am a boy with a pea-shooter; he wanted to say it aloud.

The real little boys wandered back to the hut of their own accord. They were hungry. She went up to Bam and fished, without a word, for the knife with tin-opener attachment he kept in his pocket. He noticed she gave them the last of the pork sausages, coming from the tin like plugs of wet pink cork. They snatched and quarrelled over the sharing-out. Gina was called but paid no attention; finally she walked in with the old woman's sciatic gait of black children who carry brothers and sisters almost as big as they are. She had a baby on her small back and wore an expression of importance. She sat down with her legs folded sideways under her and hitched at the dirty towel that tied the baby to her, knotted over her breastless rib-cage. She was offered a sausage; shook her head, dumb with dreamy responsibility or make-believe. No doubt his daughter was full of *pap* anyway. He and Maureen were both fascinated by her. Her eyes were crudely blue in the mask of a dirty face. Red earth engraved the joints and knuckle-lines of her little claws and toes and ash furred the invisible white fluff on her blond legs. Dirt didn't show nearly so badly on black children.

—The baby ought to go back to its mother, now.—

She countered her mother's careful reasonableness with some of her own. —Why?—

—Because babies don't like to be away from their mothers too long.—

—He *likes* it.—

—Where does he belong? Which hut?—

—Gina, which hut?—

—I don't know.—

Licking the dirt off their fingers along with the sausage grease, the boys watched the conflict with detached interest. They saw their parents closing in on one of their own kind: their father going with inescapable intention over to their sister. —Come, let's take him home.— She swivelled, zigzag-ging elbows out of his reach where he wanted to make her rise. There were yells, raised adult voices, and the baby opened one eye—the other remained stuck fast with sleep a moment—and was not alarmed at being jolted about. Just then a stick-figure danced up to the doorway and stopped dead, uncertain whether to enter. The white child threatened: —There's Nyiko! There's Nyiko!—

The black child slipped into the hut and at once the two little girls were giggling behind their hands. The black one undid the towel, threw it over her back, lifted the baby and, thrusting out her own hard bottom like a camel on its knees, saddled herself with him.

The boys saw their mother, magnanimously peace-making, was going to offer the black child one of their sausages as she left.

Maureen held it out on the point of the penknife. Before she took the food the child brought her hands together as if to pray, then opened them and cupped the palms in an attitude of receiving grace.

Maureen gave her husband back his knife without wiping it. —If only ours'd pick up the good manners along with the habits of blowing their noses in their fingers and relieving themselves where they feel like it.—

He pocketed the remark along with the knife as a sign that hostility was suspended.

The three children were locked in an endless game of tormenting one another. Because Gina lay down on the car-seat bed they shared, the boys left their contest of floating chicken feathers on currents of air and came to edge her off onto the dirt floor. The man and woman were unable to attend to the noise and appeals to their authority from both sides—there was no distraction, even in the slum propinquity of the hut they were crowded into, from their preoccupation. It grew and battened on the racket. He lay on the bed. She sat on the stool in the doorway. Now and then she came and stood beside the bed. They looked at each other.

—Want to lie down?—

But that was a *non sequitur*, like the tea she made from their precious store, pumping the Primus they'd been lent.

There was no reason why July should be expected back within any limit of time that could be fixed. She went out and gazed away over at the particular roofless hut hidden by invading trees as at the lair of some animal that has disappeared. The place looked just as it had when the vehicle had still been in there. On the bed the man kept glancing at his watch but she knew hers was a useless thing, here; yet with the deep and livid light that came flowing upon the bush from a setting sun under an inky storm-ceiling, she could not stifle a feeling of agonizing alertness. The day ending. She watched the bush; her scale pathetic, a cat at a mouse-hole, before that immensity.

When he closed his eyes he saw the hut door-opening as

the white-heat shape from a blow-torch. He could have opened his eyes on snow, snow and the safe clumsiness of figures well-insulated in bright clothing: Canada. After five years, they would have been established there by now. Muscle by muscle, his whole big body and limbs tightened upon him in a strangle-hold. If it had not been for her; he couldn't remember what he really felt he had wanted to do, stay or go, but she had a will that had twisted itself around him, he was split and at the same time held together by it as the wild fig-trees out there in the bush crack and bind rocks. He snatched up the radio and turned the knob through hellish furies of crackling, jungles of roaring, the high-pitched keening of monsters in the sizzling depths of an ocean. —For Christ sake!— She was back standing over him.

He reduced the volume and continued to play up and down the length of the band.

—There's *nothing*. You're only wasting the battery.—

He swirled suddenly to a crescendo, by mistake or in malice—her head flew up—before he put the thing aside.

—Why is it the whites who speak their languages are never people like us, they're always the ones who have no doubt that whites are superior? If we could talk— She had the slow, tight murmur of Gina when resentful.

—There's nothing significant there—don't go fishing. Not at this stage—please. I couldn't take it now. Whites in the pass offices and labour bureaux who used to have to deal with blacks all the time across the counter—speaking an African language was simply a qualification, so far as they were concerned, that's all. Something you had to have to get the job.—

—What are you lecturing about?— But he hadn't noticed he had spoken of back there in the past tense.

—I just don't want to go into a whole spiel, whether we've been deluding ourselves... If it's been lies, it's been lies.—

—Pragmatism not 'significance': that's what I'm talking about. *Fanagalo* would have made more sense than ballet.—

The shift boss Jim spoke the bastard black *lingua franca* of the mines, whose vocabulary was limited to orders given by whites and responses made by blacks. An old story that she had been ashamed—when she married her liberal young husband—of a father who had talked to his 'boys' in a dialect educated blacks who'd never been down a shaft in their lives regarded as an insult to their culture; now he, the husband, was to be submitted to her being ashamed of *that* shame. —If we'd gone five years ago, you'd have told me we'd run away. We've stayed and lived the best we could. We stuck it out— He was slowly rotating his head on his neck, as if stiffness were a noose: god knows, look at us now...

—No—*caught out.*— She would not let go; the rope might have been in her hand. —It's like when you would tell a story showing your importance or erudition and get caught out. Mmmh? Everybody listening: 'I was on the judging committee'—the architects' international award that time, when you went to Buenos Aires. Mentioning the famous names you were included among—just to claim your status without doing it in so many words. 'Most of us couldn't speak Spanish so the discussions were carried on in French'—showing that you must be able to speak French, as this was no problem for you. 'We each nominated our candidates, then we presented the laudatory argument for our choice'... I listened to you, every time. I heard you. And when someone asked who your candidates were, you couldn't answer. Couldn't remember! Had to fluff. Because what really happened was you simply enjoyed the importance of being there, being a judge, you just supported the candidates somebody else chose. And so you gave that away, too. You were caught out. *Come on.* I saw it and so did everybody. *Come on...*—

—I never believed it. But it's true, you're jealous. My god.

D'you know what this reminds me of? The time I was living with Masha, we were in the middle of having dinner at her parents' flat and she said to me when her mother got up a moment to fetch bread from the kitchen, I must tell you I'm in love with Jan (I don't remember his other name, a Pole); I slept with him this afternoon. *At the table.* Her father sitting there, but he was deaf.— He glanced at the wrangling, oblivious children. Giggled shockingly a moment; the corner of her mouth cringed at the spectacle. He held his voice rigid and violent. —You women are such bloody cowards—oh yes, physical courage, sticking it out in the bottom of the bakkie, that's something else. But you choose your moments. By Christ you do. When it comes to 'frankness'.—

—It all looks ridiculous. That's all.— Her voice came from where she had her back to him now, sitting with arms around her knees on the mud floor in the doorway, seeing the forest smudge away in darkness that stepped closer in every interval of her attention.

—What d'you bloody want to do? Conjure up Superman (he tossed open his hand at the children, who watched the serial at home) to bear them away? I know I gave him the fucking keys.—

—Why don't you admit we were mad to run. *Why can't you.*— He felt her saliva on his face. It seemed for a moment her nails would follow; he and she would fall to the ground, striking at each other in an awful embrace they had never tried. She bleated venomously: —'You wanted to go'. Why do you do what I want so that you'll be absolved.—

—What're you talking about? You wanted to get to the coast.—

—Only until he offered this. I can't stand your fucking rearrangement of facts.—

—Don't pose, Maureen. You don't have to invent yourself. That's what you accuse me of doing. You don't have to stage yourself in some 'situation' to sell to the papers when it's over. It's all minute to minute, ever since we got into that bakkie. So for Christ sake, leave it, leave it, leave us alone.—

The children had fallen asleep where they lay. He gently, ostentatiously disentangled them from the positions of conflict within which they had been overcome—Gina's cruel little hand open on the reddened ear of Royce she had been crumpling, Victor's dirt- and tear-striped cheek resting on the amulet, a large safety-pin with some beads and a fragment of hide strung on it, he had wrested from her. The fatherliness stood in for the listlessness towards the children that tension produced in their mother. Light from the paraffin lamp fell on her litter. She left them and went out; heat was darkness and darkness was heat, the moon and stars had been stifled. The bush that hid everything was itself hidden. The ringing of insects enfeebled the single, long undifferentiated cry, made up of singing, thudding, human to-and-fro that came from the convivial place where it had not ceased, did not cease. One of the strangest things about being here was that darkness, as soon as it fell every night, ended all human activity. On this night alone—Saturday—were the people awake among their sleeping companions, their animals; in the darkness (drawing away, up from it, in the mind, like an eagle putting distance between his talons and the earth) the firelight of their party was a pocket torch held under the blanket of the universe.

Heat and dark began to dissolve and she had to go in. There were no gutters; the soft rain was soundless on the thatch. Bam had balanced the stool end-up beside the iron bed and put the paraffin lamp on it. He was reading her *The Betrothed*. It was the first time there had been rain since they came; the worn thatch darkened and began helplessly to conduct water down its smooth stalks; it dripped and dribbled. Insects crawled and flew in. They were activated by the moisture, broke from the chrysalis of dryness that had kept them in the walls, in the roof. She knew that the lamp attracted them but he kept it on. The flying cockroaches that hit her face were creatures she was familiar with. There were others like outsize locusts, but shiny, with fat bodies made up of an encasement of articulated rings, that refused to die although they were beaten again and again with a shoe and a yellow paste spurted from them. These lay all over among the puddles of the floor, saw-toothed legs twitching.

He and she carried the children to the bed to keep them above the wet floor.

They sat on the car seats with the lamp hissing out time in the hot smell of paraffin. He did not read but did not put out the light: people in a hospital waiting-room in the small hours, not looking at one another. At last, deathly tiredness drained him of all apprehension; so might a man fall asleep half-an-hour before he was to be woken by a firing squad. He lay somehow on the car seat. His feet dangled. He did not know she had doused the light, the hissing, or that the rain intensified, then slackened. She went out. Night was close to her face. Rain sifted from the dark. She knew only where the doorway was, to get back. She took off her shirt and got out of panties and jeans in one go, supporting herself against the streaming mud wall. Holding her clothing out of the mud, she let the rain pit her lightly, face, breasts and back, then stream over her. She turned as if she were under a shower faucet. Soon her body was the same temperature as the water. She became aware of being able to see; and what she saw was like the reflection of a candle-flame behind a window-pane flowing with rain, far off. The reflection moved or the glassy ripples moved over it. But it existed—the proof was that there was a dimension between her and some element in the rain-hung darkness. Where it was, the rain must have thinned: and now she saw twin faint, needled beams, travelling. They progressed slowly, and because there was no other feature to be made out between her and them, seemed half-way up the sky. Then a sense of direction came to her, from the luminous trace: she stuck a pin where there was no map—there, in the dark and rain, was where the ruined huts were. The vehicle was creeping back. The point placed in her mind went back to darkness. The headlights were out, the engine off, in the roofless hut.

If it were not for the rain his voice would be carrying to her across the valley, he was a talkative man, liking to run through small events again, to savour his activity, burning accumulated garden rubbish or reorganizing storage in kitchen cupboards. No hand-held light moved; he knew his way in the dark although even the embers of the cooking-fires had been quenched by the rain.

She went in—she had kept her sopping canvas shoes on because of the dead insects—and felt her way to the dirty clothing Bam had taken off the children. She dried herself with it, put on a cardigan discovered by feel, and slept, like a drowning case in the coarse warmth of the rescuers' blanket wrapped round her, on her car seat.

Her husband was pumping the Primus. Barefoot, in his wet raincoat; must have been out to pee. The morning sounds were muffled. The children had begun to cough in their sleep for the last hour or so—the same cough that one always hears from black children. The sack was lifted and she could see the silvery hatchings of rain. He poured boiling water on tea-leaves from yesterday afternoon and while waiting for the second-hand brew to strengthen took up the radio with (secretly watching him) the baffled obstinacy of a sad, intelligent primate fingering the lock on his bars...the voice sprang out bland and clear and she was at once sitting with a straight spine.

His head was bent to the black box and his eyes caught and held hers as an admonition not to speak. '...several Sam missiles fell on the city in a rocket attack late on Friday night...Prudential Assurance Company building was the

worst hit and a fly-over on the east-west freeway suffered
heavy damage that has cut road communication...men of the
army engineering corps working throughout the night...an
attempt to take over the SABC-TV studios in Auckland Park
was repulsed by the crack commando led by Colonel Mike
Hoare, veteran of counter-insurgency against urban guerrillas in Zaïre and other African states...radio transmission was
also interrupted but the Director of the SABC has as yet is-
sued no statement...'

She slid down into her blanket again. She lay there and said
nothing of the vehicle that was once more where she was
aware of it. Her arm thrust out and he brought her the stale
hot brew in one of the pink glass cups. The distillation of
tannin drew the mouth; unconsciously she made the grimace
that appreciates the first swallow of a good whisky.

—Must have been a near thing.—

—What were you expecting to hear?—

He was drinking his tea with both hands round the small
cup. He shrugged; the strong smell of wet straw and the
damp, chilly fug of the hut was sluggishly insulating.

—'This is Radio Azania'.— She tried it out softly.

—Did you think that?—

—I don't know.— A steeple of her hands over her mouth,
the third fingers butting at her nose that was blunt and greasy
with sleep, blurred her voice. —But all the same, wouldn't it
be extraordinary...actually to hear...—

He was waiting for her to say: would we go back? They
had fled the fighting in the streets, the danger for their children, the necessity to defend their lives in the name of ideals
they didn't share in a destroyed white society they didn't believe in. Go back, at once? How to be received? Things would
quieten down—in a new way. That must be counted on. In
the Congo, Belgians went back; some of Smith's Rhodesians
stayed on in Mugabe's Zimbabwe; some Portuguese friends

returned to Maputo when Lourenço Marques no longer existed, they were prepared to live in a new way. But she didn't
want to ask the question because the hypothesis presumed,
apart from anything else, the presence of the vehicle. She kept
her knowledge of the vehicle as a possession to which she
was curiously entitled, had no incumbency to reveal. Each
one for himself. She felt no meanness in not releasing him
instantly from the anxiety they had been held in since early
afternoon the day before, and that would return to him but
not her the moment the distracting relief of bad news, over
the radio, passed. There would come a point at which she
would choose to tell him. And she would not have him asking
how, why she had come to know what she knew—silently
falsifying her taking her clothes off in the middle of the night
in the rain as some piece of psychodrama. Already he had
given a 'for god's sake?' glance of enquiry when she got up
and he noticed her thin white belly and brown pubic hair
naked below the cardigan, like some caricature of a titillating
photograph in a porn magazine, or—yes, more like—a
woman in the Toulouse-Lautrec brothel drawings they had
seen together in Europe. Before she reached that point—of
telling him (she put on her other pair of jeans, the ones from
last night were still wet, buttoned the cardigan over her
breasts and was dressed)—July's voice called at the doorway.
Bam's look was a pair of hands flung apart in the air; her
own eyes did not meet it, and perhaps he saw, in that instant,
that she had known July was back... caught out, she this time.
—You say I can come inside?— He used to have the habit
of knocking at a door, asking, The master he say I can come
in?, and they had tried to train him to drop the 'master' for
the ubiquitously respectful 'sir'. He had an armful of wood
under a torn fertilizer bag; of course (and he was right) it
would not have occurred to them to bring some wood into
shelter when the rain began. —You make small fire inside
today, s'coming little bit cold.— Royce was coughing himself

awake. —Yes, you see— The child's gaze came to consciousness on him, restfully, confident. He had dropped his city
plastic raincoat and was the familiar figure bending about
some task, khaki-trousered backside higher than felted black
head—he began at once to lay a hearth-fire.

Bam had not greeted him. Maureen was unbelieving to see
on the white man's face the old, sardonic, controlled challenge of the patron. —And where were you yesterday?
What's the story?—

July went on doing what he was expert at. The snap of
twigs, the shuffle of a single paper fist uncrumpling itself (no
cupboard full of old newspapers, here, everything that was
worth nothing must be used sparingly), a word or two to
keep Royce in bed—Little while, it's coming nice and warm,
you coming nice by the fire.—

—We were very worried.— Her implication was the flat-
tery, 'about you'.

—Where did you go?— Bam giving the man every chance
to give a satisfactory account of himself.

—To the shops.—

He straightened up and wiped his palms down his trousers.

The shops! As if he had been sent round the corner for a
pint of milk when the household ran short. The shops. The
distance to the nearest general store must be forty kilometres.
There was a police post there; certainly the Indian store
would have a petrol pump.

Bam stepped through a minefield of words before he chose
what to say. —Who drove the bakkie?—

—I got someone he's drive for me. One time he's working
there in Bethal, for the dairy, he's driving truck. He knows
very well to drive for me. I'm bring paraffin, salt, tea, jam,
matches, everything—when it's stopping to rain you come
with me, we fetch from down there.— And he patted the car
keys in his pocket.

—Did you have money?— She knew it was impossible that

he could have made free of the still-thick swatch of notes, lying swollen as the leaves of a book that has got wet and dried again, in the suitcase on which Gina, cross and unaware of anyone, as she always was in the early mornings, was sitting.

—Is fifteen rand thirty-five.— So it was he would announce the cents owed him when he had paid, out of his own pocket, the surcharge on a letter delivered by the postman while the lady of the house was out.

—Bam, we must pay July.— She shooed Gina off the suitcase.

—We'll pay. We'll pay. Did anyone see you—I mean, say anything? Ask any questions? What's happening there?—

He smiled and gave his customary high-pitched grunt of amusement when asked something obvious, to him. —Plenty people is know me. I'm from here since I'm born, isn't it? Everyone is greet me.—

—Is it quiet there? No fighting?—

He laughed. —But they tell me at the mine there's plenty trouble. People are coming home from there, they don't want to stay, they say there's burning, the houses, everything. Like in town. And the India's coming too expenses. This it's short, that it's short. Sugar... Even box matches, you must fight for get it.—

—The mine?—

Bam answered her. —There's an asbestos mine about sixty kilometres in the other direction—west. I suppose a lot of the men sign up to work there.—

—Some soldiers was coming by the shop. They tell me, last week. The India he's run away when he see them.—

—So who keeps the shop open?—

—No—(he was amused)—when the soldiers they went, the India's come back. He's there, there, in the shop.—

The little boy Royce made a dash from the bed and gained

the pillar of July's thigh. Holding on, leaning, in confused regression to babyhood, he stopped his mouth with his thumb and confronted his parents with the lowered gaze of some forgotten defiance. The black man lifted and carried the child back to bed. The parents were amiably given an order. —Just now when the rain is coming slow, I call you. I send someone, you come.— He put on the raincoat and was digging in the pockets. —Here, I bring for you— He tossed up in his palm and presented to her two small radio batteries.

—Oh how marvellous. How clever to remember.— He had heard her say it all when friends brought her flowers or chocolates.

He grinned and swayed a little, as they did. —Now you listen nice again.— It was the small flourish of his exit.

She considered the batteries in her hand; smiled at the well-meaning—not even a new battery would bring the voices from back there if the radio station should be hit.

—Put them where it's dry.—

There was only the suitcase, and even that was stained with damp moving up from where it rested on the floor. —If we could find a couple of bricks to raise it on.— But bricks were a cherished commodity; in every hut, they were used to raise beds. Where was Bam to find bricks for her? She found her own solution. —Ask July.—

She was quite competent at making porridge, now. It was the little community's own meal, grown by them and stamped by the women in big wooden jars. It looked more like bits of coarse broken yellow china than the sugar-fine grains commercially milled. It tasted better, too, than the packaged stuff, rough as it was. Everyone knew that; it was sold in health shops and eaten by white food-faddists with honey and butter... Salt! He had brought salt, at least. That was what had been missing, now she would be able to put salt in the water in which she boiled the meal.

People—black people—would certainly have seen him at the store, in possession of the yellow bakkie.

—So he turns up there as if the millennium has already arrived.—

She was stirring the meal thickening on the Primus. Spoon dripping in her hand, she looked at Bam, considering what could be done for him rather than what he had said. —But jam will be good—a dollop of jam with this...— She stirred as if to shift their energies. —He did bring things.—

There was the moment to ask him for the keys. But it was let pass.

They stood in the midday sun and watched, over at the deserted dwelling-place, the yellow bakkie being reversed, bucking forward, leaping suddenly backwards again; kicking to a stop. July was at the wheel. His friend was teaching him to drive.

After days of rain hot breath rose from everything, the vegetation, the thatch, the damp blankets of all patterns and colours hung out over every bush or post that would spread them. Submission to the elements was something forgotten, back there. You shivered, you had no dry clothes to replace wet ones. The hearth-fire that filled the hut with smoke was the centre of being; children, fowls, dogs, kittens came as near to it as the hierarchy of their existence allowed. The warmth that food brought—blood chafing into life—came from it, where the clinkers of wood, transparent with heat, made the porridge bubble vigour. Bam and Maureen had longed for cigarettes, for a drink of wine or spirits, their children had craved for sweet things; but in the days of rain, the small fire they never let die satisfied all wants.

A shimmer of heat like a flock of fast-flying birds passed continually across the movements of the vehicle. He was getting the hang of it.

When the lesson petered out he and his friend sat about on their hunkers—too far away to make out what they were doing; just talking, no doubt, July stimulated and eager to communicate, as everyone is when acquiring a new skill, the stages at which mastery eluded or came to him. Walking back through the valley, he waved jubilantly when he was near enough to recognize and be recognized.

—I would never have thought he would do something like that. He's always been so *correct*.— Bam paused to be sure she accepted the absolute rightness, the accuracy of the word. —Never gave any quarter, never took any, either. A balance. In spite of all the inequalities. The things we couldn't put right. Oh, and those we could have, I suppose.—

Gratitude stuffed her crop to choking point. —We owe him everything.—

Her husband smiled; it didn't weigh against the keys of the vehicle, for them.

Oh, she didn't deny that. She was setting out the facts before herself, a currency whose value had been revised. It was not only the bits of paper money that could not supply what was missing, here.

—I'd give him the keys any time. I could teach him to drive, myself—he hasn't asked me. All right—someone has to get supplies for us...—

—As long as the money lasts.—

—The money! We'll be out of here, with plenty of

money.— Habit assumed the male role of initiative and reassurance—something he always had on him, a credit card or
cheque-book. She would not look at him, where it had passed
from him, and remark his divestiture.

July's wave had been innocent. He came with their supply
of wood—all still so damp, the whole settlement was hazed
bluish from everyone's cooking-fires, once more established
outdoors. Bam spoke up with independent pleasantness.
—You shouldn't bother. I've told you. I can chop my
own wood. You mustn't do it.—

—The women bring the wood. You see all the time, the
women are doing it.— It was an issue not worth mentioning; he was enthusiastic about his prowess with the vehicle.
—You know I'm turning round already? I'm know how to
go back, everything. My friend he's teaching me very nice.—

—I saw. You didn't say you were going to learn to drive.
You never said you wanted to learn.—

—In town?— He was affable, deprecating his own ability,
or reminding that they knew he had known the limits of his
place.

—Here. Here.—

He leaned forward confidentially, using his hands. —Is no
good someone else is driving the car, isn't it? Is much better
I myself I'm driving.—

—If they catch you, without a licence...—

He laughed. —Who's going to catch me? The white police-
man is run away when the black soldiers come that time.
Sometime they take him, I don't know... No one there can
ask me, where is my licence. Even my pass, no one can ask
any more. It's finished.—

—I'm still worried that someone will come to look for us
here because of the bakkie.—

—The bakkie? You know I'm tell them. I get it from you
in town. The bakkie it's mine. Well, what can they say?—

Only a colourless texturing like combings from raw wool across the top of his head from ear to ear remained to Bam—he had begun to go bald in his twenties. The high dome reddened under the transparent nap. His eyes were blue as Gina's shining out of dirt. —Is it yours, July?—

All three laughed in agitation.

—They hear me. They must know, if I tell them I take it from you.—

A wave of red feeling—it seemed to flash from Bam's fine pate to her—sent her backing them all away at a warning. Again, she gained foothold, spoke from there. —Martha's given me something for the children's coughs. She makes it out of herbs—at least, she showed me some plants she was boiling—

July's eyes at once screwed up. —What? She's give you what? That stuff is no good. No good.—

—But she gave it to the baby. Your baby. That's how I could show her I wanted something for Gina and Royce—Royce never stops, all night, although he doesn't wake up.—

His face was flickering with something suppressed: annoyance with his wife, irritation at responsibility—he was not a simple man, they could not read him. They had had experience of that, back there, for fifteen years; but then they had put it down to the inevitable, distorting nature of dependency—his dependency on them. —That medicine is no good for Royce. You don't give that for Royce. You give it already?—

—No, I thought tonight. I thought maybe it's something that makes you sleepy—

—It's—you know... It's not for white people.—

She was smiling as if he knew better. —Ju-ly...your baby is given it. Don't tell me it can do any harm.—

—What do they know, these farm women? They believe anything. When I'm sick, you send me to the hospital in town. When you see me take this African medicine?—

—Well, all right. But even in town plants are used for some cough medicines. It might have helped. I haven't anything to give him.—

—Me, I'm try next time I'm go to the India shop.—

Bam put an end to an academic argument. —There won't be medicines. Grandpa Headache Powders, maybe.—

—No, he's right, they'll quite likely have some sort of cough syrup, think of all the chest troubles rural people get, living like this. It's possible.—

—Royce he's coming warm enough in the night? I think I bring blanket I got there in my house.—

She shook her head, smiling thanks. Swiftly, she placed—not a request, an assumption. —I'm going to put the rubber floor-mat from the bakkie under where he sleeps.— Her hand was out.

—I wanted to fetch it this morning, but you've kept the keys.— Bam did not raise his voice; had never shouted for him, back there. The white man (Bam saw himself as they would see him) would walk out into the yard, reasonably, when there was a reproach to lay at the door of his room, where his friends, so well-dressed on their days-off, sat gossiping.

—Who will go to the shop to get things for you? Who can bring your matches, your paraffin. Who can get the food for your children? Tell me?—

She always took on the responsibility of assuming herself addressed; she was the one who understood him, the way he expressed himself.

—*Of course.* I'll bring them back to you.—

—Tell me?—

—Of course, yes of course.—

He looked at her, looked away. —Tomorrow I'm go get medicine for Royce. That child he's sick.—

He turned around in the hut a moment as a man does when he forgets what he is there for. Falling in step with some pattern chanced upon he began to push about the small, crowded, darkened space, dragging and shaking things into a private order.

They stood there while his obsession swirled about them. They looked neither at him nor at each other; at least they did not allow themselves to be driven out along with the fowls, the nuisance of whose droppings was equalized by the benefits of an assiduous scavenging for the insects who shared the hut.

There was in his dark profile, the thrust of the whites of his eyes suddenly faced and away again, the painful set of his broad mouth under the broad moustache, a contempt and humiliation that came from their blood and his. The wonder and unease of an archetypal sensation between them, like the swelling resistance of a vein into which a hollow needle is surging a substance in counterflow to the life-blood coursing there; a feeling brutally shared, one alone cannot experience it, be punished by it, without the other. It did not exist before Pizarro deluded Atahualpa; it was there in Dingane and Piet Retief.

A sudden leaping, punching broke the air outside.

Victor and his gang of boys raced chattering upon the doorway.

—Everybody's taking water! They've found it comes out the tap! Everybody's taking it! I told them they're going to get hell, but they don't understand. Come quick, dad!—

The black faces of his companions were alight with the relish of excitement coming, the thrill of chastisement promised for others.

—But it's their water, Victor. It's for everybody. That's what I put the tank up for.—

The child scratched his head, turned out his muddy bare feet and tottered round on the heels, clowning. —Ow, dad, it's ours, it's ours!— His friends were enchanted by the performance and began their own variations on it.

—Who owns the rain?— The preachy reasonableness of his mother goaded him.

—It's ours, it's ours.—

July was instantly affectionate, playful, light and boastful with the boy. —You lucky, you know your father he's very, very clever man. Is coming plenty rain, now everybody can be happy with that tank, is nice easy, isn't it? You see, your father he make everyone-everyone to be pleased.—

Always a moody bastard.

The term was not a strong one, in her observations to herself; there were times when she remarked her small daughter behaved to Victor and Royce 'like a real little bitch'.

She had indulged him, back there. She had been afraid—to lose him, the comforts he provided; to be inconsiderate of private sorrows he might have she might know nothing of, and that she could guess at only in the shape of circumstances into which he didn't fit. Did he love the town woman? She thought of that, here. And did that mean he would have liked to bring the town woman here and live with her permanently?

The humane creed (Maureen, like anyone else, regarded her own as definitive) depended on validities staked on a belief in the absolute nature of intimate relationships between human beings. If people don't all experience emotional satisfaction and deprivation in the same way, what claim can there be for equality of need? There was fear and danger in considering this emotional absolute as open in any way; the brain-weighers, the claimants of divine authority to distinguish powers of moral discernment from the degree of frizz in hair and conceptual ability from the relative thickness of lips—they were vigilant to pounce upon anything that could be twisted to give them credence. Yet how was that absolute nature of intimate relationships arrived at? Who decided? 'We' (Maureen sometimes harked back) understand the sacred power and rights of sexual love as formulated in master bedrooms, and motels with false names in the register. Here, the sacred power and rights of sexual love are as formulated in a wife's hut, and a backyard room in a city. The balance between desire and duty is—has to be—maintained quite differently in accordance with the differences in the lovers' place in the economy. These alter the way of dealing with the experience; and so the experience itself. The *absolute nature* she and her kind were scrupulously just in granting to everybody was no more than the price of the master bedroom and the clandestine hotel tariff.

She had in her hand one of the clay oxen Gina was learning to make, that had been set to dry in the sun. Abstractions hardened into the concrete: even death is a purchase. One of Bam's senior partners could afford his at the cost of a private plane—in which he crashed. July's old mother (was she not perhaps his grandmother?) would crawl, as Maureen was watching her now, coming home with wood, and grass for her brooms on her head, bent lower and lower towards the earth until finally she sank to it—the only death she could afford.

Maureen had the keys, kept overnight after she had fetched the rubber mat from the vehicle. She heard his voice, his energetic laugh, and saw him cross from hut to goat-kraal and back. To be seen is not necessarily to be acknowledged, where people's movements are centred about the same kind of activity in every household, every day. Everyone was everyone else's witness, and this bred its own discretion. Only the children hung together and moved like the comet's tail of bees she had seen roll out of the sky the other day and bear down on tree after tree before attaching itself to one. She had never been inside his hut; Bam had. —He has some things from home. It's smartened-up. He can't live like the others.— Bam meant the home he and she had provided; he meant the wife and female relatives.

She rehearsed her arrival at the door of his domain. It was only a hundred feet away. His quarters had been only across the yard, she had waved at his friends, his brothers who were eternally visiting, seen through the open door in summer, or heard them in there, round the electric heater she provided, in winter—she came right by his quarters every time she went to the double garage to drive off in her car. But she had never entered unless—rare occasion—he was sick. Then she knocked, and the attendant friends stood up respectfully (accommodated somehow on up-ended boxes, an old table—she provided one decent chair for her servant's comfort but could not be expected to allow for the reception of half-a-dozen friends), and she would put down on the spotless bed the tray of light food she had prepared for him herself. His hut, here, was apparently something he kept to himself, apart from women. But she was a white woman, someone who had employed him, theirs was a working relationship; surely that was her claim.

She had lived for more than two weeks within steps of that hut and could have lived there for ever without going inside it. She no more wanted to have to see her cast-off trappings here, where they separated him from the way other people lived around him, than she did back there, where they separated him from the way she lived. The old green bedspread with dolphins, mermaids and tritons printed round a fake facsimile of an early map of the world, the framed poster of Málaga—these things themselves (in his room back there) might not be displayed, but others of the same origin. He must have known, when she handed some new object on to him it was because it was shoddy or ugly, to her, and if it were some old object, it was because she no longer valued it. She stopped Royce (his favourite) who kept running past to help himself and the other children to the peanuts that were Victor's share of the harvest Victor had helped dig up: —See if you can find July.—

Her child came back with his troop. They lay belly-down on their elbows on the damp ground and crowded heads blissfully over their cracking of tiny fibrous shells. —Did you find July?—

—Mmm. There at his house.—

—Is he coming?—

—He says it's all right, he's there, you can come.—

She sat on in the sun that crisped the skin, a hot iron passing over damp cloth. She was menstruating—since the day before, although by the calculation of the calendar left behind above the telephone it would have been a week too soon. There was another essential she had forgotten. Under her jeans she wore between her legs the wadding of rags that all the women here had to when their days came. Already she had been, with the modesty and sense of privacy that finds the appropriate expression in every community, secretly down to the river to wash a set of bloody rags. She had no thought for the risk of bilharzia as she scrubbed against a stone and watched the flow of her time, measuring off another month, curl like red smoke borne away in the passing of the river.

—Want some?— Her youngest child still needed to share his pleasures with her.

Red earth and bunches of raw peanuts clung to the roots of the plants.

—If you don't eat them all, I'll roast the rest. With salt.
Then they have some taste.—

—Same as in the packets? In the shops?—

—That's right.—

—I didn't know those grew!—

The little boy's toes drummed at the earth and while he ate
he hummed, as he would soon cease to do, becoming too old
to find content between his lips, as he had at her nipple. He
seemed to understand what the black children said; and at
least had picked up the ceremonial or ritual jargon of their
games, shouting out what must be equivalent of 'Beaten you!'
'My turn!' 'Cheat!'

—Go and say I want to see him.—

The whole formation of children took off. She put out a
hand and a black head with the feel of freshly-washed sheep-
skin brushed under it. Sometimes she could coax a small
child, new on its legs, to come to her, but mostly she was too
unfamiliar-looking, to them, to be trusted.

The children did not return. She thought she heard him
singing, way up in the bones of his skull, the hymns he
breathed while he worked at something that required repeti-
tive, rhythmical effort, polishing or scrubbing. But when he
appeared he was merely coming over to her, unhurried, on a
sunny day. Nothing sullen or resentful about him; her little
triumph in getting him to come turned over inside her with a
throb and showed the meanness of something hidden under
a stone. These sudden movements within her often changed
her from persecutor to victim, with her husband, her children, anyone.

She spoke as she did back there when domestic detail im-
pinged upon the real concerns of her life, which could not be
understood by him. But she had got to her feet. —Here are
your keys.—

For an instant his hands sketched the gesture of receiving

and then were recalled to themselves and the thumb and fingers of his right hand simply hooked the bunch, with a jingle, from her fingers.

His chin was raised, trying to sense rather than see if Bam was in the hut behind. Her silence was the answer: not back; they both knew the third one had gone off, early, to shoot some meat—a family of wart-hogs had been rashly coming to an old wallow within sight of the settlement. He stood there, his stolidity an acceptance that he could not escape her, since she was alone, they were one-to-one; hers an insinuated understanding that she had not refused to come to him but wanted them to meet where no one else would judge them. The subtlety of it was nothing new. People in the relation they had been in are used to having to interpret what is never said, between them.

—You don't like I must keep the keys. Isn't it. I can see all the time, you don't like that.—

She began to shake her head, arms crossed under her breasts, almost laughing; lying, protesting for time to explain—

—No, I can see. But I'm work for you. Me, I'm your boy, always I'm have the keys of your house. Every night I take that keys with me in my room, when you go away on holiday, I'm lock up everything...it's me I've got the key for all your things, isn't it—

—July, I want to tell you—

The ten fingers of his hands, held up, barred what *she* thought, *she* wanted. —In your house, if something it's getting lost it's me who must know. Isn't it? A-l-l your things is there, it's me I've got the key, always it's me—

—July, you don't ask me—

—Your boy who work for you. There in town you are trusting your boy for fifteen years.— His nostrils were stiff dark holes. The absurd 'boy' fell upon her in strokes neither appropriate nor to be dodged. Where had he picked up the weapon? The shift boss had used it; the word was never used in *her* house; she priggishly shamed and exposed others who spoke it in her presence. She had challenged it in the mouths of white shopkeepers and even policemen. —Trust you! Of course we trusted you—

They had moved closer together. She put a fist, hard claim, upon his arm.

—No. No. You don't like I must have these keys.—

—July you don't ask me—you're just telling me. Why don't you let me speak? Why don't you ask me?—

He drew his head back to his steady neck, to look at her. —What you going to say? Hay? What you can say? You tell everybody you trust your good boy. You are good madam, you got good boy.—

—Stop saying that.—

—She speak nice always, she pay fine for me when I'm getting arrested, when I'm sick one time she call the doctor.— He gave a laugh like a cry. —You worry about your keys. When you go away I'm leave look after your dog, your cat, your car you leave in the garage. I mustn't forget water your plants. Always you are telling me even last minute when I'm carry your suitcase, isn't it? Look after everything, July. And you bringing nice present when you come back. You looking everywhere, see if everything it's still all right. Myself, I'm not say you're not a good madam—but you don't say you trust for me.— It was a command. —You walk behind. You looking. You asking me I must take all your books out and clean while you are away. You frightened I'm not working enough for you?—

—If you felt I shouldn't have asked you to clean out the bookshelves that time, why didn't you say so? What were you afraid of? You could always tell me. You had only to say so. I've never made you do anything you didn't think it was your job to do. Have I? *Have I?* I make mistakes, too. Tell me. When did we treat you inconsiderately—badly? I'd like to know, I really want to know.—

—The master he think for me. But you, you don't think about me, I'm big man, I know for myself what I must do. I'm not thinking all the time for your things, your dog, your cat.—

—*The master.* Bam's not your master. Why do you pretend? Nobody's ever thought of you as anything but a grown man. My god, I can't believe you can talk about me like that... Bam's had damn all to do with you, in fifteen years. That's it. You played around with things together in the tool shed. You worked for me every day. I got on your nerves. So what. You got on mine. That's how people are.— She flowered into temper. —But we're not talking about that. That's got nothing to do with now. That's over—

He flickered his eyes. —How you say it's over—

—Over and done with. You don't work for me any more, do you.—

—You not going pay me, this month?—

—Pay you!— She glowed and flashed. He continued a kind of fastidious pretence of insensitivity to a coarse and boring assault. —You know we can pay you what you used to get, but we can't pay you for—

—African people like money.— The insult of refusing to meet her on any but the lowest category of understanding.

—You know quite well what I mean... For what's happened. It's different here. You're not a servant.—

—I'm the boy for your house, isn't it?— He made a show of claiming a due.

—What's the good of going on about that? It's six hundred kilometres over there—her arm flung across before his face the useless rope of a gesture that would fall short of what had disappeared into the bush. —If I offended you, if I hurt your

dignity, if what I thought was my friendliness, the feeling I
had for you—if that hurt your feelings...I know I don't know,
I didn't know, and I should have known— The same arm
dangled; she didn't know, either, if he understood the words;
she dropped fifteen years of the habit of translation into very
simple, concrete vocabulary. If she had never before used the
word 'dignity' to him it was not because she didn't think
he understood the concept, didn't have any—it was only the
term itself that might be beyond his grasp of the language.
—If I ask you for the keys now it's not the key of the kitchen
door! It's not as a servant you've got them. Is it? But a
friend—he asks, he asks...and he gives back...and when he
wants something again, he asks again.—

He produced the keys in his palm. —Take it. It's not the
keys for your kitchen. Fifteen years I'm work for your
kitchen, your house, because my wife, my children, I must
work for them. Take it.—

—If all you can think about is what happened back there,
what about Ellen?—

The name of his town woman fell appallingly between
them, something neither should dare take up.

—What is happening to Ellen? Your wife and your children were here, and all those years Ellen was with you.
Where is she, in the fighting there? Has she got something to
eat, somewhere to sleep? You were so concerned about your
wife—and what does she think about Ellen?—

He had stopped instantly the blinking pantomime of deri-
sion. He might take her by the shoulders; they stepped across
fifteen years of no-man's-land, her words shoved them and
they were together, duellists who will feel each other's breath
before they turn away to the regulation number of paces, or
conspirators who will never escape what each knows of the
other. Her triumph dissembled in a face at once open, sub-
missive, eyes emptied for a vision to come, for them both.

He shuddered in affront and temptation; she saw the convulsion in his neck and understood he would never forgive her the moment. Her victory burned in her as a flame blackens within a hollow tree.

A servant replied uninterestedly to a dutiful enquiry on the part of the good madam who knows better than to expose herself to an answer from the real facts of his life: —I think Ellen she's go home to her auntie there in Botswana. Small small village. Like my home. Is quiet there for black people.—

He put the keys in his pocket and walked away. His head moved from side to side like a foreman's inspecting his workshop or a farmer noting work to be done on the lands. He yelled out an instruction to a woman, here, questioned a man mending a bicycle tyre, there, hallooed across the valley to the young man approaching who was his driving instructor, and who was almost always with him, now, in a city youth's jeans, silent as a bodyguard, with a string of beads resting girlishly round the base of his slender neck.

The white man had watched the wart-hog family shifting through the grasses, appearing as the aerials of raised tails, then cropping nearer and nearer each afternoon as they fed, the adults' coarse hairy backs gleaming with glistens of mud from the wallow. It was a sight for tourists in a game reserve; drink in hand, legs crossed at the picture window of an air-conditioned bungalow.

There were five young, two grown females and the big male with his cow-catcher tusks on a snout that was, in fact, shaped rather like an old steam railway-engine. The blacks had no guns and feared the tusks; the pigs concentrated on feeding and showed no more than the usual deep, general distrust of beasts for humans, following whatever it was, plant or grass, that attracted, nearer and nearer to the huts, and then, at the lift of a head (one of the sows or the boar) running up the pennant of tail and turning about to trot off swiftly. Their heavy bodies bounded like corseted women. At that, the tourists laugh; the ugliness clowns the dignity, the dainty trot the overweight—these are 'adorable' creatures.

Bam pulled the gun out of the rotten thatch and appeared with it before July's villagers. He did not know everyone knew he had the gun; that the children who made free of every hut as the cockroaches, knew everything and chattered all. He walked among them harmlessly; look, he and his gun were theirs. Some of the women smiled, most ignored him. There was a trail of children led by his own son Victor, beating sticks and boasting. July had always kept superstitiously clear of shot-guns; unpacking the hunting gear in the backyard after his employer returned from a trip, he would put the gun-cases straight into the hands of Bam with the slow, gingerly movements of finger-tips singed by fear. All to the good, that way he didn't throw them about and damage them. But his friend wearing a necklace showed the interest that claims some technical knowledge. He wanted to hold the gun; Bam showed him how to aim at a moving target and explained the loading mechanism. —Have you ever fired a shot?—

The young man shook his head and others laughed at white ignorance. —I read about it.— In the present tense. So he could speak a little English, the ex-milkman. Whether he read gangster comics or had read some crude clandestine sheet on handling firearms...? Such sheets had been circulating in the most unexpected, remote areas of the country over the past ten years—at every political trial of blacks the State produced them in evidence of subversion. But with the sweetness and freedom that came from powerlessness (for the time being, until they got out of here) Bam was almost flippant. —I'll let you try sometime. What's your name?—

—Daniel.— He pointed towards himself the gun that was back in Bam's hands until the barrels were looking him right

in the eyes, two blue-steel tunnels with an immaculate bur-
nish, a precision of echoing roundness spinning away with
the light that whirled along them—something more perfect
than any object in the settlement or that he had ever seen,
anywhere. He concentrated a long moment, imposing respect
against frivolous interruption. Then he released himself with
a small sound, inconclusive, disbelieving. Perhaps he didn't
credit death could be so clean; thought he had looked it back
in the eye; perhaps he was too young to believe it existed.

Bam waited hidden near the hog wallow. He had with him
one youngster of about fourteen he had appointed. He had
had to cast about in his mind for something to threaten or
promise that would keep Victor behind at the settlement—
his kind did not strike their children and it was difficult to
deprive the child of some treat or privilege here, in penalty
for disobedience, as so easily could be done at home. —I
promise you I'll let you have the skin. We'll get one of July's
relations to teach us how to preserve the skin.—

—And if you don't get anything?— The boy yelled after
him. —What'll you give me if you don't get anything?—

The father did not look up. Pushing through tongues of
wet grasses with his gun, with a youth metamorphosed into
the quickness and hesitancy of a buck, beside him—half
in the familiar experience of his weekend pleasures from back
there, half in the jarring alertness of these days broken from
the string of his life's continuity and range, *minute to minute*,
his legs taking him where a patrol or roving band might come
upon him, the shots he was going to fire risking to give away
the presence of a whole family of whites, hidden in those
huts—disjointed by these contrasting perceptions of habit
and strangeness, he had a foretaste of the cold resentment
that he would feel towards his son sometime when he was a
man; a presentiment of the expulsion from a paradise, not of
childhood but of parenthood.

He waited in the reeds with the young black face frowning in wretched endurance of the mosquitoes. The wart-hogs came and he fired at the nearest piglet when they were in the position from which they would have the least chance of getting away. A rifle, not a shot-gun, was the weapon for these beasts; all he could do was use buckshot and hope it would be heavy enough to penetrate their hide. All the old games, the titillation with killing-and-not-killing, the honour of shooting only on the wing, the pretence of hide-and-seek invented to make killing a pleasure, were in another kind of childhood he had been living in to the age of forty, back there. The first piglet dropped and he got another, seconds slow to disappear after the adults into the bush. The boy who had been a buck became a predator, leaping onto the first piglet; then a hunter, tying its legs together with one of the bits of string, used over and over, that were treasured in every hut. The animal was quite still, already, dying fast with the settling of sight in its eyes on some point that wasn't there. The other piglet was hit in the body and lying kicking in a tantrum of pain; or thought its waving legs were carrying it after the big safe bodies of the adults. The black boy, with the first beast neatly trussed to his hand, squatted to wait for the other to die. Bam waved him aside and shot it through the head. Its young bones were so light that the snout smashed. It was horrible, the bloodied pig-face weeping blood and trailing blood-snot; the clean death from the chromed barrels that smelled aseptically of gun-oil. Game-birds (his usual prey) had no faces, really; thin aesthete's bony structure with its bloodless beak and no flesh, a scrap of horny skin, wrinkled paper eyelids—a guinea-fowl head doesn't look much different, dead, from alive. The shattered pig-face hung to the ground, dripping a trail all the way back to the huts, where his function as a provider of meat settled upon him as a status.

He was aware she might remark upon or sympathize with the necessity. He put up an off-hand taciturnity against this. He understood, for the first time, that he was a killer. A butcher like any other in rubber boots among the slush of guts, urine and blood at the abattoir, although July and his kin would do the skinning and quartering. The acceptance was a kind of relief he didn't want to communicate or discuss.

But Maureen stood by with her hands on her hips. Her calves and feet, below rolled-up jeans, were dirty as a hobo's. —Give them the bigger one.—

He didn't need advice on justice or the protocol of survival.

She murmured for his ear alone. —The small one will be more tender.—

He took only a side of the smaller pig, and the skin for Victor, neatly headless. A man whose oedematous flesh kept him immobile, standing shaped like a black snowman (he always wore a dirty muffler against a bubbling chest ailment) or propped on an old chair, an effigy of straw stuffed in old clothes, had come to life and chopped off the broken head. He looked around jealously and carried it away to hands that received it into the darkness of a doorway, his great soft thighs shuffling as the breasts of the women did while they pounded mealies.

Bam rigged up a spit. Lacking herbs, onion or pepper— only the salt Maureen massaged over the firm skin—the meat was a feast never tasted before. They and their children had not eaten wart-hog, and they had never before gone two weeks without meat. The incense of roasting flesh—there was not much fat, only the domestic swine runs to that—rose from every cooking-fire. There were dog-fights roused by the mere smell of it. The half-wild, half-craven cats clamoured incessantly on the periphery of Maureen's preparations. She squatted, carefully basting the carcass with the juices it gave off into an old powdered-milk tin she held, a stick's length away from her, among the flames. Sweat and smoke swam across her vision and now and then she staggered up for a respite, laughing at herself, while Bam took over.

They had not known that meat can be intoxicating. Eating animated them in the way they attributed to wine, among friends, around a table. Bam sang a comic song in Afrikaans for Royce. —Again! Again!— Gina wavered through a lullaby she had learnt from her companions, in their language. Victor became a raconteur, past, present and distance resolved in the best tradition of anecdote: —You know what we do at school? On Friday when the big boys go to cadets, and they're not there to boss us around in the playground—

There were drunken, giggling accusations of boasting, lying; and swaggering denials. The children made the grown-ups laugh. Royce hummed and sucked on the pipe-stem of a rib-bone; was almost asleep. Carried off in a state of unprotesting confusion to be bedded-down, he mumbled with content. —There's no school tomorrow, is there?— It was what he would ask, sometimes, on a Friday evening, when he was allowed to stay up late.

They had not made love since the vehicle had taken them away. Unthinkable, living and sleeping with the three children there in the hut. A place with a piece of sacking for a door. Lack of privacy killed desire; if there had been any to feel— but the preoccupation with daily survival, so strange to them, probably had crowded that out anyway. Tension between them took the form of the expectation of hearing a burst of martial music when they turned on the radio. It subdued into the awkward sense of disbelief, foreboding, and immediate salvation (lucky to be alive; even here) that came from the announcement of the battle for the city that was continuing, back there.

They were conscious of the smell of grease and meat clinging to their fingers. It was difficult to balance, in the space each kept to of the car seats they shared, without folding elbows and resting hands near one's face. They made love, wrestling together with deep resonance coming to each through the other's body, in the presence of their children breathing close round them and the nightly intimacy of cockroaches, crickets and mice feeling-out the darkness of the hut; of the sleeping settlement; of the bush.

In the morning he had a moment of hallucinatory horror when he saw the blood of the pig on his penis—then understood it was hers.

Good meat, *mhani?*—
        The old woman was at an age when people pretend not to enjoy anything, any more, as a constant reproach to those who are going to live on after them.
        —When was the last time you had such good meat?—
        She twitched away from a subject not worth her attention.
—Meat is quickly gone. You eat it, there's nothing again to-morrow. My house has to have a new roof, the rain comes in. And in the winter it'll be cold. I was going to put on new grass...—
        —You'll put on your new grass.—
        She made a face of calculatedly reasonable questioning, to her son.
        —You'll have your house, your new grass.—
        —With them living in it.— His wife Martha was scouring with ashes an enamel pot that came packed in his luggage the leave-before-the-last. —Heyi, *mhani!*—

—I'll build you a new house. You see? You worry about this business—but I'll build you a new one.—

—They will bring trouble. I don't mind those people— what do they matter to me? But white people bring trouble.— The woman drew a husky song from the pot, rubbing away at it, not looking at him so that she would not attract his annoyance.

He drummed out what he was always having to repeat. —What trouble? From where?—

She knew she could not say to him as she had said before: trouble with the police, the government.

He half-laughed, half-grunted; made as if to leave the two women to their goading ignorance, then turned, glancing thoughts off them like stones skimming water. —If I say go, they must go. If I say they can stay...so they stay.—

His wife persisted, as her fingers did with the daily tasks— hesitating, picking over dried beans, working the paste of ash over the pot—putting together the past from the broken pieces brought before her by the yellow bakkie. Her voice took the tone of simple curiosity. —There in town, the white woman—did she say to you you must cook this or clean that—

—Nobody else can tell me. If I say—

She was shaking her head, down, to herself; it was as if he were not there. It was habitual to address him when he was not there, he had been gone so long, her conversations with him provided question and response out of her own brood- ings. Sometimes he disappeared completely; she was not aware of his existence, anywhere. It was then she dictated letters to him through someone who could write better than she could (although she could read his, written in their own language, she had not had much other need to write since her three years at school and the ball-point she kept for this pur- pose formed words that staggered across the ruled pad): *My dear husband, I think all the time of the days you were here and when you will come again.* Most of the women of child-bearing age had husbands who spent their lives in those cities the women had never seen. There was a set of conventions for talking about this. The man had written or had not written, the money had arrived or was late this month, he had changed his job, he was working in 'another place'. Was there anyone, some other woman whose man had perhaps worked there, someone to whom the name of yet another town none of the women had ever seen, was familiar? It did not so much as occur to her that it could have been possible to talk to other women about what was asked in the conversations with her husband that never took place. Not even to her man's mother, who was old and had that in her face which showed she would know the answers; she had had a man thirty years on the mines.

Across the seasons was laid the diuturnal one of being without a man; it overlaid sowing and harvesting, rainy summers and dry winters, and at different times, although at roughly the same intervals for all, changed for each for the short season when her man came home. For that season, although she worked and lived among the others as usual, the woman was not within the same stage of the cycle maintained for all by imperatives that outdid the authority of nature. The sun rises, the moon sets; the money must come, the man must go.

His wife had the power of a whingeing obstinacy, shying away and insisting. —No, there in town. Was it the man who told you what you—

It was hardly worth answering. —You know I didn't make the food. There was the Xhosa woman, the cook.—

—How must I know, I didn't see her—

—Nomvula. The one they called Nora. You saw her on the photo. One Christmas. You got the photo they took of us.

With the children, Gina and the boys. A coloured picture. You've got it. Albert brought it with the shoes I sent.—

The old woman completed the description. —The fat woman with a pink cap like this— (She cocked a hand over one eye.) —Looks as if she likes to drink.—

—Was she married?—

—I think her husband died.—

—So she didn't have a man?—

She watched him for an answer. She saw he was thinking of something else, back there. The backyard photograph, the white man and woman and their children here and now— the concrete knowledge of these was hers but provided too scanty a trail for her to follow him by.

—There's Bongani. The Zulu, he works as an inspector for the Cleansing Department. Dressed up in a uniform on his bicycle. He stays with Nomvula in her room.—

—They didn't mind him living in the yard... Mnnn. And what happened to Nomvula? Where did she go now?—

He sat down on the small low bench placed inside the hut against the wall, where male strangers sat when they came to visit. The single source of light, from the doorway, axed the interior diagonally; on the one side, women, the planes of the bay of mud plaster behind them lifted into ginger-gold, richly-moted relief like the texture of their faces, on the other, the man in darkness. His hands were on his knees. They could see his fingernails and his eyes. Perhaps he had shrugged to show he didn't know. When his wife had assumed he wasn't going to bother to answer—and she didn't need an answer, anyway; the Zulu was the answer that satisfied her, her further question was a distraction of others' attention from that satisfaction—he spoke from his corner. —I don't know where she is. What happened to her. If she reached her family in...— His voice trailed off, confused, as if he had forgotten a place-name; or could not speak it.

The clay vessels Maureen used to collect as ornaments were now her refrigerator and utensils. Vermin, fowls, weak and savage cats who tailed her openly or secretly for their survival, scenting food on her hands, hearing the proximity of food in her footsteps, domestic pigs who followed her in the hope of picking up her excrement, were reinforced in numbers by the birth of a litter to one of the cats. The creature settled itself on the haversack Bam used as a pillow. He tipped her gently off. Gina and Victor brought a plastic-net sack of the kind in which oranges were sold, back there, and substituted it as a nest for the litter. But a man came with the face of aggrieved sullenness that was familiar, the face that had been appearing for generations at the back door, asking for but not expecting to get justice, only the redress of a handout. Maureen knew who he was; she had watched him, passing time for herself in silence with what passed it for him, as he unravelled the synthetic fibre of an orange-sack, smoothed it into lengths and knotted, then plaited these to make a strong, bright rope. The couple made out that he wanted the sack back; the children had stolen it.

Victor's look went from mother to father like a hand to a holster. —It was lying around! A whole lot of them, just lying around under a tree. We just took it!—

Gina was aghast at the enormity of the accusation as she had been at tale-telling at school. —An old orange-bag! Who's going to steal a bit of rubbish! Anyway, *we* brought a bag of oranges, didn't we, ma, didn't we, one of those old bags is *our* bag. *This* is our bag, one of them's *ours*, isn't it. How can you steal something that's thrown away?—

—But those orange-sacks are something he uses for his work, Gina—

—What can he use them for? What 'work'?—

—He makes rope. They're his material.—

Victor was angry with a white man's anger, too big for him. —He mustn't say I stole. I just took stuff that gets thrown away, nobody wants—

But all the parents did was give the man a two-rand note, and Bam patted him on the back with gestures of apology and assumption that adults must make allowances for the actions of children.

Victor stood giddy with the force of spent emotion, after the man had gone. —Gee, two rands for an old orange-bag. I could buy one of those vintage buggy miniatures for that. *I'll* get him some old orange-bags if he'll pay me two rands.—

His father laid the same calming hand on him, a palm lightly on his head. —If he had two rands to pay for an old orange-bag, he'd be able to buy a rope instead, wouldn't he.—

Royce made his way patiently round the whole question to approach his brother shyly, confidentially. —You going to buy one of those little buggies, Vic? I mean, if you get two rands?—

—Where can you buy them. Here. They had them in Sandton, at Pick 'n Pay. That's where you get them.—

—Ask July, Vic. Why don't you ask July? Vic?—

Emotion suddenly came back to the boy; his lids reddened. —Well, one thing—I know one thing, not all Africans are nice like July. Some of them are horrible. Horrible.—

Nyiko, Gina's friend, who slipped in and out the hut all day as the passing fowls did, had come in and gone straight to Gina in the lover-like seclusion of childhood intimacy. They stood hand-in-hand, looking mildly on at Victor's suffering. Gina pulled a kitten for each of them from the cat's teats and the minute creatures were possessed by a tension of claws and mewling as much too great for them as the boy's anger had been for him.

There came the expected admonition from a parent—the mother. —You must not keep taking them away from the cat. They're only two days old.—

The father spoke to the mother in the sub-language of hints and private significance foreign to the children. —Maybe Nyiko knows whose cat it is? Perhaps we can give the whole bang-shoot where it belongs.—

She looked at him; token acknowledgement given to someone who speaks from a premise that doesn't exist.

Through Gina, he questioned Nyiko. The little girl giggled. She crinkled her nose and showed her teeth; and was asked again. Gina waggled the hand in hers. Nyiko giggled and swayed from foot to foot. —Daddy, she doesn't understand. She says nobody's got a cat.—

—I see, I see. *Everybody* has cats, just as cats have fleas.—

The little girl was impatient of his flirtatious fondness. —No-*oo*, I told you. Nobody's got one...she says.—

In the afternoon he went to fish at the river. He and his

family couldn't bring themselves to eat barbel but the other people appreciated them. He left the children down there and came back in time to listen to the four o'clock news. *She* was lying on the bed; any one of the hut's occupants who found himself in sole possession for an hour would at once take the opportunity of having the use of the bed. He saw her; saw himself as he was when he sometimes lay there; and thought of the prisoner as he is always visualized in his cell. He himself had become able to sleep at will, since he had been in this place: will himself out of it, away from her, from the children, waiting for him to get them out of it.

No martial music.

They listened to the news. The reception was bad, the reader a stumbling speaker—who was left, at the state broadcasting service's splendid towers of granite, to do such a job? Possibly the transmission no longer came from there—the service had always concealed so much, it probably would never announce it had been forced to evacuate and was operating from some temporary hideout. The hard-pressed but stolidly bureaucratic-sounding reports quoting 'authoritative sources': was the Brigadier of the Citizen Forces, in whose name an assessment of the success in 'containing' Soweto from the Diepkloof Military Base was given, one who had in reality run like anyone else? Was the eye-witness account of the recapture of the Far West Rand mines—so haltingly putting together the description of a rout that didn't seem to fit the features of a landscape natal to the daughter of My Jim Hetherington—a Bunker fantasy? Such reverses that were incontestably admitted were so ominous; last night the Union Buildings in Pretoria were 'partially destroyed'. No mention of a rocket attack, this time. The pile must have been blown up from within, they were probably actually fighting with their bodies and hands over Sir Herbert Baker's colonial grace in pillars and sandstone. Or maybe they had blown it up themselves rather than let blacks move in.

It had become impossible to talk about what was happening, back there. He and his wife listened in silence and he noted subconsciously something trivial that he could remark on when the radio was switched off. —Did you find someone to take the kittens?— They were no longer in the hut.

She got up sluggishly from the bed; she certainly had been taking a nap.

—I drowned them in a bucket of water.—

She used sometimes to answer him outlandishly, out of sarcasm, when he suggested she might do something it was beyond question—by nature and intelligence—for her to have done. *Now don't let slip to Parkinson I don't intend to go to the meeting because I've no intention of voting, mmh.* —Oh *I've already had a good chat with Sandra about it, just to be sure he'll get to hear.*

This kind of repartee belonged to the deviousness natural to suburban life. In the master bedroom, sometimes it ended in brief coldness and irritation, sometimes in teasing, kisses, and love-making of a variety suggested by the opportunities of the room and its rituals—a hand between her legs while she was cleaning her teeth, the butting of his penis, seeking her from behind while she bent over the bath to swish a mixture of hot and cold water.

She was lean, rough-looking—the hair on her calves, that had always been kept shaved smooth, was growing back in an uneven nap after so many years of depilation. That she had said 'in a bucket': he understood that as it was meant, a piece of concrete evidence of an action duly performed.

—Oh my god.— His lips turned out in disgust, distaste, on her behalf.

She scratched efficiently at her ribs, working the shrunken T-shirt against the bones just below her shallow breasts.

—Oh my poor thing.—

She pulled the shirt over her head and shook it. To lie down was to become a trampoline for fleas. —What're you making a fuss about.— The baring of breasts was not an intimacy but a castration of his sexuality and hers; she stood like a man stripped in a factory shower or a woman in the ablution block of an institution. —I used to take them to be spayed.—

—Well of course you took them to be spayed.—

—Obsessed with the reduction of suffering. It was all right, I suppose. ...Not how to accept it, the way people do here.—

—I should damn well hope not.—

Her neck was weathered red and over-printed with dark freckles down to a half-circle bisected by a V, the limits of the T-shirt and cotton blouse which were her wardrobe. He would never have believed that pale hot neck under long hair when she was young could become her father's neck that he remembered in a Sunday morning bowling shirt.

The tight T-shirt dragged back down her features, distorting eyes, nose and mouth. It was as if she grimaced at him, ugly; and yet she was his 'poor thing', dishevelled by living like this, obliged to turn her hand to all sorts of unpleasant things. —Why didn't you get one of them to do it?—

At first the women in the fields ignored her, or greeted her with the squinting unfocused smile of those who have their attention fixed on the ground. One or two—the younger ones—perhaps remarked on her to each other as they would of someone come to remark upon them—a photographer, an overseer (at certain seasons they had used to hire themselves out as weeders on white farms, being fetched by the truck-load from many miles distant). She followed along, watching what it was they selected, picked and dug up—July's mother, in particular, seemed to have a nose for where her pointed digging-stick would discover certain roots. She herself could not expect to acquire that degree of discernment but could recognize wild spinach and one or two other kinds of leaves she saw the women bend for and put in their baskets. When her hands were full, she dropped what she had garnered into one of these. Then she found herself an old plastic bag that had once contained fertilizer—people brought home whatever could be scavenged when they went to the dorp or worked on the farms—and tied it with a bit of string to hang from her shoulder, as those who did not have baskets did.

The sun brought the steamy smell of urine-wet cloth from the bundles of baby on the mothers' backs. The women hitched up their skirts in vleis and their feet spread, ooze coming up between the toes, like the claws of marsh-birds; walking on firm ground, the coating of mud dried matt in the sun and shod them to mid-calf. She rolled her jeans high, yellow bruises and fine, purple-red ruptured blood-vessels of her thighs, blue varicose ropes behind her knees, coarse hair of her calves against the white skin showed as if she had somehow forgotten her thirty-nine years and scars of child-bearing and got into the brief shorts worn by the adolescent dancer on mine property. July's unsmiling wife was laughing; looking straight at those white legs: she did not turn away when Maureen caught her at it. Laughing: why shouldn't she? July's wife with those great hams outbalancing the rest of her—Maureen laughed back at her, at her small pretty tight-drawn face whose blackness was a closed quality acting upon it from within rather than a matter of pigment. Why should the white woman be ashamed to be seen in her weaknesses, blemishes, as she saw the other woman's? For a while they worked along a donga like a team, unspokenly together, now side by side, now passing and repassing each other, closely; then July's wife was hailed by somebody a little way off, and moved on about her business, as every woman did, individually, yet keeping the pattern of a flock of egrets, that rises and settles now here, now there, where the pickings are best.

The family ate their share of the greens with mealie-meal. If he—Bam—knew she had gathered them herself, he said nothing. But when Victor demanded more greens, he answered him swiftly. —You've had your share. It takes a lot of effort to get them.— Turning the dry *pap* in her mouth she had a single throb of impulse, quickly inert again, to go over to the man and sink against, embrace him, touch someone recollected, not the one who persisted in his name, occasionally supplying meat, catching fish for people.

The news: that day the station was impossible to tune into under the hooting racket of jamming and for the first time they found themselves listening to what could only be MARNET, the Military Area Radio Network, that had been developed originally to supplement vulnerable telephone communications on the border in the Namibian war, and lately extended to the whole country. The voices were employing a code, but there were direct references to Diepkloof, the military base between Soweto and Johannesburg. The abrupt urgency of Afrikaans voices was suddenly lost; like the impulse. She watched him fiddling with the knob and trying to find the transmission again. He kept his back to her as if he were doing something private and shameful. He had switched off; and took possession of the bed.

She walked out into the vacuum of the hot afternoon without any objective, bothered by a veil of flies. Thatch, old tins, cock's plumage glittered drably: she made for the place where the yellow bakkie was hidden, only because it was *somewhere else*—there was nothing belonging to her, in the vehicle, any more. Ants had raised a crust of red earth on the dead branches that once had formed a cattle-pen. With a brittle black twig she broke off the crust, grains of earth crisply welded by ants' spit, and exposed the wood beneath bark that had been destroyed; bone-white, the wood was being eaten away, too, was smoothly scored in shallow running grooves as if by a fine chisel. She scraped crust with the aimless satisfaction of childhood, when there is nothing to do but what presents itself; wandered on; there the vehicle was, still there.

A pair of legs in Bam's old grey pants stuck out from beneath it.

There is always something to say: the formula for the roadside breakdown. —What's the trouble?—

July's voice came between grunts. —No, is coming all right. That pipe, like always, it's little bit loose—

—Oh the exhaust. Well, it took a bashing getting here. Can't expect anything else.—

He worked himself out, along the earth, on his back, blinked and shook his head to get rid of the dirt that had fallen on his face. Smiling, made a deep clicking exclamation of comic exasperation: —That thing!— He questioned someone, in their language; Daniel was still under there.

July got stiffly to his hunkers. His greasy hands hung by the wrists. —At home we had that strong wire.—

She nodded. A roll—far too much, more than they could ever have put to use, taking up space in the double garage between the sack of charcoal for the braais, and the lawn mower.

He laughed. —Man, I wish I can have some of that wire here!—

—I wonder if there's anything left.—

—Ye-s-ss! Everything it's there! When we go I'm putting that big (he mimed the padlock with first finger and thumb hooked across the knuckle of the other hand) I'm closing up nice!— He leaned his back against the wheel of the bakkie. Pride, comfort of possession was making him forget by whose losses possession had come about.

—The fighting must be very bad.—

—You heard something what they say?—

—Not the radio we always hear. I think that's finished. Maybe the building is blown up—I don't know. The special radio, for the army.—

For him, too, there had always been something to say: the servant's formula, attuned to catch the echo of the master's concern, to remove combat and conflict tactfully, fatalistically, in mission-classroom phrases, to the neutrality of divine will. —My, my, my. What can we do. Is terrible, everybody coming very bad, killing... burning... Only God can help us. We can only hope everything will come back all right.—

—Back?—

She saw he did not want to talk to her in any other way.

—Back?—

His closed lips widened downwards at each corner and his lids lowered as they did when she gave him, back there, an instruction he didn't like but would not challenge. —I don't want to hear about killing. This one is killing or that one. No killing.—

—But you don't mean the way it was, you don't mean that. Do you? You don't mean that.—

Daniel, young and lithe, rolled easily from under the vehicle and stood by. She glanced to him for agreement, admittance to be extracted by the two of them. He too, had something to say to her: a greeting, *ihlekanhi, missus.* July spoke to him. A few half-attentive questions were followed by some sort of order given: in any case, the young man was propelled by it down into the valley, going off in the direction of the settlement, maybe to fetch something for the repair-work.

But as soon as he was ten yards off they both knew it was a pretext to get him out of the way. Maureen felt it had been decided she had come to look for July; helpless before the circumstantial evidence that they were now alone, again, as they were when he came to the hut and she was aware he was looking behind her to see if anyone was inside.

She might just have come into his presence that moment; he spoke as if opening a conversation out of silence, as if they had not already been talking. —I'm getting worried.—

She knew his use of tenses. He meant 'am worried'.

—You are hungry. I think you are hungry.—

She smiled with surprise; and suspicion. —Why d'you say that? We're not hungry. We're all right.—

—No... No. You have to go look for spinach with the women.—

The answer came back at him. —I go. I don't have to go.—

—If the children need eggs, I bring you more eggs. I can bring you spinach.—

—I've got nothing to do. To pass the time.— But they could assume comprehension between them only if she kept away from even the most commonplace of abstractions; his was the English learned in kitchens, factories and mines. It was based on orders and responses, not the exchange of ideas and feelings. —I've got no work.—

He smiled at the pretensions of a child, hindering in its helpfulness. —That's not your work.—

She had had various half-day occupations over the years; he used to shut the gate behind her—a wave of the hand, lingering to talk to his passing friends in the street—when she drove away to her typewriter, newspaper files, meetings, every morning. Yet he knew she could work with her hands. When the shift boss's daughter had dug and planted all Saturday in the garden he would (it seemed to her then) acknowledge her comradely: —Madam is doing big job today.— Now he chose what he wanted to know and not know. The present was his; he would arrange the past to suit it.

—Anyway, I don't want the other women to find food for my family. I must do it myself.— But here they both knew the illusion of that statement, even while they let it stand. July's women, July's family—she and her family were fed by them, succoured by them, hidden by them. She looked at her servant: they were their creatures, like their cattle and pigs.

—The women have their work. They must do it. This is

their place, we are always living here and they are doing all things, all things how it must be. You don't need work for them in their place.—

When *she* didn't understand *him* it was her practice to give some noncommittal sign or sound, counting on avoiding the wrong response by waiting to read back his meaning from the context of what he said next. (Despite his praise of Bam—was it not given to wound her rather than exalt Bam?—Bam did not have this skill and often irritated him by a quick answer that made it clear, out of sheer misunderstanding, the black man's English was too poor to speak his mind.) He might mean 'place' in the sense of role, or might be implying she must remember she had no claim to the earth—'place' as territory—she scratched over for edible weeds to counter vitamin deficiency and constipation in her children. She didn't wait to find out. She spoke with the sudden changed tone of one who has made a discovery of her own and is about to act on it. —I like to be with other women sometimes. And there are the children, too. We manage to talk a bit. I've found out Martha does understand—a little Afrikaans, not English. It's just that she's shy to try.—

The pleasant smile of her old position; at the same time using his wife's name with the familiarity of women for one another.

He settled stockily on his legs. —It's no good for you to go out there with the women.—

She tackled him. —Why? But why?—

—No good.—

The words dodged and lunged around him. —Why? D'you think someone might see me? But the local people know we're here, of course they know. Why? There's much more risk when Bam goes out and shoots. When you drive around in that yellow thing... Are you afraid— Her gaze sprang with laughing tears as if her own venom had been spat at her; he and she were amazed at her, at this aspect of her, appearing again as the presumptuous stranger in their long acquaintance. —Are you afraid I'm going to tell her something?—

Giddied, he gave up a moment's purchase of ground. —What you can tell?— His anger struck him in the eyes. —That I'm work for you fifteen years. That you satisfy with me.—

The cicadas sang between them. Before her, he brought his right fist down on his breast. She felt the thud as fear in her own.

It echoed no other experience she had ever had. The shift boss with his thick, miner's wrists and stump where the right third finger had caught in a kibble underground would never cross the will of his little dancer; her husband—what could ever have arisen, back there, that would make him a threat to her? And here; what was he here, an architect lying on a bed in a mud hut, a man without a vehicle. It was not that she thought of him with disgust—what right had *she*, occupying the same mud hut—but that she had gone on a long trip and left him behind in the master bedroom: what was here, with her, was some botched imagining of his presence in circumstances outside those the marriage was contracted for.

She had never been afraid of a man. Now comes fear, on top of everything else, the fleas, the menstruating in rags— and it comes from this one, from *him*. It spread from him; she was feeling no personal threat in him, not physical, anyway, but in herself. How was she to have known, until she came here, that the special consideration she had shown for his dignity as a man, while he was by definition a servant, would become his humiliation itself, the one thing there was to say between them that had any meaning.

Fifteen years

   your boy

     you satisfy

She walked away and sat on a mud ruin, sending her gaze far from them—from him, from her—over the grey and green bush, a layer of cumulus seen from a jet plane between two continents, where crossed date-lines eliminate time and there are no horizons.

The clink and wrench of tools on metal was taken up against the single continuous note of the cicadas. Her broken nails—only the left thumbnail, always hornier and harder than the rest, retained semblance of the oval it was kept to back there—could not score the earth wall. When she lifted and looked at her palms they were stippled with the pressure of the grains but carried none with them; in the veld round the mine, she had stubbed her toes again and again on the same hard dark earth, bonded into anthills. She got up and went to where he had dragged the exhaust pipe from the bakkie and was tinkering with it between his spread legs.

He had never been any good with mechanical things.

Look at the pliers he was using. Even she could see they were too small to grip properly.

And he was approaching the task from the wrong angle.

The pipe should be the other way up. Bam remarked how, if July packed the car, the suitcases were placed upside down, standing on their lids. She wouldn't have Bam say anything to him, offend his pride—he was so highly intelligent in other ways.

He persisted with pliers and screwdriver; got no message from the awkward stress between metal and his fingers. He never had; what problems with the lawn mower, half-dismantled, and left in the yard until Bam came home.

Oh not that way. Even a woman can tell that.

Her presence conveyed all this to him, in their silence both heard, knew from what had been unspoken in their past.

She said it. —You've never been able to fix machines. Get Bam to do it. Ask him.—

He didn't answer. He didn't know 'Bam', a white man from whom he had taken the vehicle; like her, he knew someone left behind back there, the master who would put together the pieces of the lawn mower when he came home. But he silenced her: —Yesterday night someone's come.—

The whip cracked over her head. Deep breaths slowly pumped her chest; she was aware of the pulse showing in her small, flat, left breast under the T-shirt: fear, in there. —Police? Who came?—

He left her to it a moment. —Someone there from the chief.—

Relief made her impatient. —Well that's all right, July, isn't it—he knows you. I mean he must know you've got somebody here.—

—He know who is it me... He send someone ask who I'm keep in my house. Someone say you must come there to the chief's place, I must show him. Always when people is coming somewhere, they must go to the chief, ask him.—

—Ask him what?—

—Ask him nice, they can stay in his village.—

—I thought you said this is your place, everybody knows it's your place, you can do what you like. You've been saying that since we arrived. A hundred times.—

—Yes, I'm say that. *My* place it's here. But all people here, all villages, it's the chief's. If he's sending someone ask me this or this, I must do. Isn't it. If he's saying I must come, I must come. That is our law.—

—Why didn't you tell us before, if the polite thing—if it's nice to go and see the chief?—

He looked up: her dirty feet, her thin face from which the hair was drawn back in a rubber band. The colour had worn off her jeans along her thighs and fly. —Now I'm tell you.—

—When?—

He gestured; in his own time. —Tomorrow.—

—Bam can go with you.—

He was carrying on with his repair. —You, master, your children. All is going.—

She was unsteady with something that was not anger but a struggle: her inability to enter into a relation of subservience with him that she had never had with Bam. Leave it, she said of the vehicle, as she had said of her lawn mower. —Leave it. He'll come and fix it.—

She started off towards the settlement. On the descent she turned, against the sun a moment, as if she would call back. Then she came purposefully to where she had stood before. They were near each other. Her eyes hooded by her hand, his head under the vehicle, neither could see the other's face. She said what nobody else should hear. —You don't have to be afraid. He won't steal it from you.—

Bam rose from the bed like a man who has fallen asleep on the couch in his office when he was supposed to be working.

—It's a question of courtesy, apparently. I don't think there's anything sinister. Paying respects to the chief.—

He was surly at feeling ridiculous. The haversack that was his pillow had made a deep crease on one cheek. His unused voice snagged on phlegm. —Ours is hardly a state visit here.—

—Anyway, we have to go. I don't know why he didn't say so before.—

—Didn't you ask?—

—He wasn't prepared to be forthcoming. In a bad mood.—

—What's the matter?—

She had picked up their water-bottle as she came in and

was gulping straight from the neck between speaking. Her mouth was wet, she grinned with the voluptuousness of thirst quenched. —He's afraid I'll tell about his town woman.—

—He's what?—

—Because I've got friendly with Martha—the wife—you know. Well *friendly*, hardly—we exchange a few words in the fields, she can speak a bit of Afrikaans, I've found out.—

—Oh, his Ellen. But what makes him think you would?—

She looked at this half-asleep man who did not know. She spoke violently, if not to him. —It's rubbish. Don't let's transpose our suburban adulteries. His wife knew nothing else about him, there, either.—

Bam tore off a length from one of the toilet rolls she had not forgotten to provide, and went out into the bush. He left the smell of his sweaty sleep behind him; she had not known, back there, what his smell was (the sweat of love-making is different, and mutual). Showers and baths kept away, for both of them, the possibility of knowing in this kind of way. She had not known herself; the odours that could be secreted by her own body. There were no windows in the mud walls to open wide and let out the sour smell of this man. The flesh she had caressed with her tongue so many times in bed—all the time it had been a substance that produced this. She made a cooking-fire outside and the smoke was sweet, a thorny, perfumed wood cracking to release it. The others—Martha— were wise to keep the little hearth-fire alive always in the middle of the huts. Only those still thinking as if they were living with bathrooms *en suite* would have decided, civilizedly, the custom was unhygienic and too hot.

In the morning they were ready to go. In clean, un-ironed clothes they were shabbier than July and Daniel; Maureen would not attempt to use one of the old flat-irons, heated in the fire, with which the women made a perfect line of fold down the legs of frayed and ragged trousers. She was talkative, joking affectionately with the children, smiling, over their remarks, complicity with him—Bam; like she used to be when they were off on a family outing, to the drive-in cinema or a picnic. They had been shut up in the vast bush that surrounded them for more than three weeks: any move into it was an occasion. He himself felt an urge to shave; he did so irregularly, now. Even the prisoner, when the day comes for him to face the dreaded charge in court, probably is excited by being piled into the Black Maria for the drive along city streets scented and glimpsed behind steel mesh; Bam had seen the fingers sticking through it, while passing prison vans in his car, back there.

He had in his breast not dread—a lump of certainty. The chief wanted them to move on; the three children running in and out the hut with their childish sensationalism, their plaints, their brief ecstasies, his wife knocking a nail into her sandal with a stone, and he, shaving outside where there was light. Would tell them to go. What business of the chief's to tell them where? He had not asked them to come here. A wide arc of the hand: plenty place to go. And this was not *their* custom, but the civilized one; when a white farmer sold up, or died, the next owner would simply say to the black labourers living and working on the land, born there: go.

He said nothing of this certainty to her not because of any wish not to alarm her—the male chivalry of the suburbs had no right to keep her in ignorance of what she had to fear and it could not defend her against—but because he did not know to whom to speak these days, when he spoke to her. 'Maureen'. 'His wife'. The daughter of the nice old fellow who had worked underground all his life and talked of the stopes of Number 4 Shaft, the heat in Number 6, the 'bad luck' his boys felt (long before he lost his finger there, in that section of Number 4 where the kibble caught him), as a man talks fondly of the features of the town in which he grew up. The girl in leotards teaching modern dance to blacks at night-class, under the eyes of her architect boy-friend with his social conscience. The consort clients meant when they said: And we'd so much like you and your wife to come to dinner. The woman whose line of pelvis, shifting backside, laugh among other people sometimes suddenly became strongly attractive again after fifteen years; that same woman familiar as a cup on the kitchen shelf. The woman to whom he was 'my husband'. The other half in collusion, one for purposes of income tax, one to provide an audience at school sports, one in those moments when, not looking at each other, without physical contact or words, they clasped together against whatever threatened, in the nature of menace there was back there—professional jealousy, political reactionism, race prejudice, the wine-tasting temptation of possessions.

Her. Not 'Maureen'. Not 'his wife'. The presence in the mud hut, mute with an activity of being, of sense of self he could not follow because here there were no familiar areas in which it could be visualized moving, no familiar entities that could be shaping it. With 'her' there was no undersurface of recognition; only moments of finding each other out. For the children she chose to appear as 'their mother', 'his wife', this morning. But she was no one to whom he could say that the chief was going to tell them to go. He had no idea how she would deal with his certainty. There was no precedent to go on, with her. And he himself. How to deal with it. How to accept, explain—to anyone: after all these days when his purpose (his male dignity put to the test by 'Maureen', 'his wife', Victor, Gina, Royce, who were living on mealie-meal) had been how to get away—now it was how to stay.

Daniel was surely unnecessary but he was of the party; neither he nor she suggested the young man should be left behind. The placing of the children in the bakkie had to be rearranged several times before everyone was satisfied. July did it, as he used to do the suitcases. The children obeyed him, anyway, although he made none of the parents' attempts at fairness, he openly favoured Royce. Daniel got into the back with them and at once was claimed in rivalry as a playmate. Gina had wanted to bring Nyiko along; she took him of right, as a substitute, yelled in his own language, which she was learning in the form of 'private talk' between Nyiko and herself, He's *my* friend, mine!

Maureen opted out of the children's wrangle and settled herself in the middle of the front seat, where she would travel between driver and second passenger.

The door was open on the driver's side. He went round to the other but July was there before him and got in. There was a moment's pause but July was not looking his way. He went under their eyes—Maureen, July—past the hood of the vehicle and climbed in behind the steering-wheel. The rim had been adorned with a plastic clip-on cover printed with a leopard-skin pattern. That couldn't have come from the Indian store. More likely a garage 'boutique' somewhere. (He slid a glance, half-smile, to her; she stared round abruptly at his profile: what did he want?)

Maybe July, like Maureen, had taken to looting.

July signalled, his arm raised, fingers of the hand folded together in a goose's head, jabbing: straight on, straight on. The vehicle followed cattle tracks. Thorns screeched across the windows. Cows with long, deformed horns drew together to watch the yellow object approach and July wound down the window and put out his arm to bang a warning with the flat of his hand on the body-work. The vehicle passed huts where people were doing what they did where the passengers had come from. The same endless dragging of wood, chopping of wood, for the same fires; the same backsides bent at washing, squatting picking over maize; the same babies staggering towards mastery of their legs among the old slowly losing it. An acceptance that produced restless fear in anyone unused to living so close to the life cycle, accustomed to the powerful distractions of the intermediary or transcendent— the 'new life' of each personal achievement, of political change.

People looked up at the load in the bakkie with faces of those seeing for themselves something they had heard about. Once or twice July called out a greeting.

—No main roads, eh, I hope.—

—Never!— July laughed. —We are coming now-now.—

The vehicle slowed over the bare grazed ground that marked each settlement; they were again among a few huts, fences made of rubbish, green scrolls of pumpkin patches. Half-turns to right and left were ordered; right-angles belong back there, with street-signs and numbers. Even the bakkie had some difficulty negotiating the gullies in the public way.

—Slow slow.—

—This is it?—

July spoke with a dreamy reassuring tolerance of others' nerves. —We just going stop that place under the tree. Just wait little bit there by that building there. Over there.—

They sat in the vehicle.

He read in her silence an old expectation—didn't apply any more—that he would ask the man to give account of his actions: July had jumped down and shut the door on anyone who thought to follow. He would scarcely be needing to ask the way; was this perhaps the chief's house?

To them, a church or schoolhouse—the kind of utility structure, a 'building' rather than a large hut by virtue of its brick construction and rectangular shape, about which Bam had once presented a paper (*Needs and Means in Rural African Architecture*). Not every community could afford the tin steeple or peak-roofed porch entrance early missionaries had decreed—apparently God couldn't live in a black man's round house. The place had a tin roof and two pairs of windows with cardboard patching broken panes. There was a length of angle-iron hanging from a tree—the usual substitute for a church- or school-bell, struck when it was time for children or congregation to assemble. But no cross anywhere, and instead of the dust patch with rough-dressed goal posts that was every school's sports facilities, there was this grassy open space, with hitching posts under two trees of ceremonial size and dignity that had been spared any loppings for firewood. Three horses tied up; a man lay on his back splattered by the shade of the tree his shoulders rose against. Daniel must have brought a radio with him; the heavy beat and plea of pop music swarmed out from the back of the vehicle.

He left the driver's seat and went round to the rear hatch.
—What's this place?—

Royce and Victor were pelting each other with some kind of hard seed-pod. Gina leaned on Daniel with her small hand at the tuning knob, smiling majestically, the blare and rhythm an extension of her body. —This place?— Daniel laughed at him, searching for the words he would understand. —This place it's the—the *hubyeni*. It's where the people...they come.—

He got back into the vehicle and ran a five-finger exercise up and down the mock leopard-skin on the steering-wheel. —The Great Place. Chief's Great Place. That must be the court-house. They will have held the *kgotla* under those jakkalsbessie trees. Once.—

—Then why don't we go in?—

—How should I know?—

After the silence he spoke again. —Let him handle it. He's always been a shrewdy.—

There was some reaction of hostility in her, an emanation. But they had been in it together, 'Maureen', 'his wife'; she knew that. They had been amused together at July's calculation, on strips torn from the margins of their newspapers, of his ten-cent bets and one-rand gains in the Fah-Fee game he acted as agent for, from their backyard. When gently teased, he had a way of rubbing first finger and thumb together. Grinning: *Everybody he's like money.* Of course—Shylock's gesture from a man so poor he had nothing to offer in the city but his own pound of flesh, and nothing else to gain there beyond money; money in the beggarly denominations a servant knows.

The music had given way to a voice with the same urgent, triumphant, cheerful cadence used by disc-jockeys everywhere, reading the news in Portuguese. The transmission must have been coming from Moçambique, but there were recurrent mentions of 'Azania Freedom Fighters' in English, a repetition of place-names, Pretoria, Johannesburg, and Bam could make out several references to the American Embassy. He stuck his head through the window to hear better, then jumped out of the vehicle again. He took the radio from the child but the newscast ended, he had missed the last of it in the noise the children were making. The man from under the tree had wandered over to gaze at them all and talk to Daniel. He was bare-foot, with a fighter's furrowed thick face and a wall eye that seemed constantly to be trying to get away from what it saw. Daniel and the local were talking about him, the white man, as he stood there holding the radio and trying to get some other station; talking over him as people talk over the supine man in his hospital bed. The little girl jigged a passion of possession for the transistor; music vibrated again. As he turned back to the cab of the vehicle, July was approaching with a man whose advance was formal and belly-first. He wore a collar and tie and a suit made up of odd-matched jacket and trousers. He suddenly paused, leaving July to go on unnoticingly a few steps ahead, and drew back a round shaved head on a thick smooth neck, screwing up one side of his face at the sight of the bakkie and those inside it. Then he came heavily on, as if through crowds in a path cleared for him by July.

A good thing there had not been time to get back into the vehicle; it would be disrespectful not to be standing for this meeting. But July seemed to be fumbling his part, attempting no introduction—well, perhaps—what could he say? *Chief, this is the Master.* (How many times, back there, had Maureen and Bam tried to get him to drop the Simon Legree term, but he wouldn't, couldn't, as if there were no term to replace it, none that would express exactly what the relationship between Bam and him was, for him. Yet when some friend of the house occupied the guest room or was invited to Sunday drinks and supper, the servant who was also a familiar would exchange with the white man or woman easy greetings and superficial family news.) The big black man murmured deeply and hastily over a formula of greeting (they wouldn't understand, anyway) whose tone contradicted, authoritatively, any welcome or acceptance.

—Bamford Smales. My wife...our children.— He put out a hand and the other took it. The process of weighing up a presence—the yellow bakkie, the white man outside the vehicle and the woman and children inside—was like a form of digestion, audible in the sounds the man made without words. The clearing of his throat was a rap for attention. —You coming from where?— July must have told him, he must, like everyone else around, have known of their presence and their story; this was the magisterial ritual of cross-examination.

—Johannesburg, with July.—

—I see, I see...— The jaw lifted consideringly and strongly from its bed of fat and the eyes sized the contents of the vehicle once more, acknowledging a greeting from the woman by a tremor of flesh-swags under the chin. Daniel, once driver of a milk truck in town, got out giving the raised fist greeting of the black townships, and stood ignored, roughly aligned with July.

—And you are coming here. For what are you coming?—

A smile—unconscious attempt to be ingratiating; if one knew what would please...?—a hand run over the pate where there were only fine, short blond hairs left, the skin was not pleasant to touch, scaly from exposure to the sun. —Well, you know the trouble there. It's like a war. It is a war. We could have been killed. The houses where we stayed...they've been burned, bombed—some of them. People had to leave, our children might have been hurt. July brought us.—

July interrupted. —He tell me the chief's in his house. We go there to the chief's house now.—

The big man's gait was suddenly recognizable as that of a city doorman or (to her, certainly) an *induna* who would sit on guard on his fruit-crate outside the compound where the shift boss's labourers lived. That must have been why she hadn't got out of the bakkie as 'his wife', to stand beside 'her husband'. Anyway, he shook hands with the man again before they drove on.

—What was he? I mean, what does he do?—

It seemed always to amuse July to be the mentor, as if he didn't take too seriously a white's wish to comprehend or faculty of comprehension for what he had never needed to know as a black had the necessity to understand, take on, the white people's laws and ways. —Headman. He's headman for the chief.—

—Really headman, or are there more than one?—

Laughter again. —Sometime is plenty, is plenty villages.—

—A headman for each village?—

—Ev-'ry village. But this one is headman for the chief. Same village like where the chief he's live.—

She took up her old role as interpreter. —Don't you see? The headman of all the headmen. A personal assistant, adviser—I don't know—to the chief.—

He steered the yellow bakkie in the spaces between mud huts, people and animals. The rag flags of religious sects and those that were the professional plates put up by *sangomas*, men and women who foretold the future and interpreted the past by throwing bones, stood out in bright, store colours on wattle poles outside some huts. There was a collapsing wattle stall with an advertisement for Teaspoon Tips Tea nailed to it, but nothing displayed for sale. He spoke to her alone.
—We should have brought something.—
—A case of gin and the promise of a gun-boat?—
—A bottle of whisky.— The kind of goodwill gesture it was permissible to make towards a good client, or the gift he would take to a farmer in return for the hospitality of a shooting weekend. It could hardly be expected to change the mind of the black man who had the right and authority, here, to tell them to go. But if he had thought of it, if July could have found a bottle somewhere (the Indian store-keeper wouldn't sell drink), he would have told him to buy one.
—There was something about the American Embassy.—
—But in Portuguese. Might have had to do with another part of the world.—
—No, I could make out...there were references to Pretoria and Johannesburg.— He had brought the vehicle to a stop where July indicated: a group of the usual huts, one that had a crude porch—wattle poles with a sheet of corrugated tin. A girl of about twelve swung a baby boy out of the way, by his arm, little moles of breasts nosing up from her dark flesh. Johannesburg, Pretoria; as much another part of the world as anywhere else that might have been mentioned.
They all got out of the vehicle and stood in the shade of the tin roof. Round each support the earth had washed away forming a circular depression whose rim was hard and smooth as and the colour of toothless gums. Everything in these villages could be removed at the sweep of a bulldozer

or turned to ashes by a single match in the thatch; only the earth, worn to the bone, testified to the permanence of the feet that abraded it, hands that tamped it, hearth-fires that tempered it. Flies were drowning in a black pot crusted with mealie-meal set to soak off in water. A man came from the doorway—too dark to see in unless one went close up, which visitors couldn't do—and talked to July, went back inside again. A woman with spirals of white hair standing up over her head theatrically (they customarily covered their heads with *doeks* or caps) carried out a tin basin and emptied dirty water with a twang. When she had done it, she turned to Daniel, who referred her to July; she questioned him and was answered with all his repertoire of amiable, thoughtful, lively, deferential cadences and exclamations. Another man came up; the first appeared again. The conversations died away like songs. There was nothing to be done but wait. The children tried to fondle the usual cats, but the cats were terrified of human hands and hid behind an old car radiator grid whose honeycomb was welded with rust. Victor wanted to know if his father would buy it. —It's a real Morris, it's from the wire-wheel model. Oh come on, dad, man, *ask*. If they'll sell it. But just *ask*.—

He felt unable to answer his son. There was a car seat (not from the same car) and Maureen had plonked down on it; how everything came easily to her now, if she didn't know what was expected of her she did as she liked. He put himself beside her. Before an operation for piles he had waited like this on a trolley in the hospital corridor, his feet cold and his mind held just above anxiety by some drug he had been given, or maybe merely by the business of waiting and the uselessness of any volition.

He got to his feet suddenly. A man had appeared in a group of those already seen and July and Daniel had at once fallen to their knees and folded their hands. The thin man's body had none of the city African's ease inside his clothes. How to recognize a black chief in the same sort of cast-offs other rural blacks wore? But a new snap-brimmed hat rested just above irritable veins raised in sunken temples.

He towered, clumsy and blond, bald, before the chief he was being presented to. The chief shook hands with him, his woman, tactfully ignored the children, who were entranced, between laughter and queer awe, at the sight of July and Daniel. Their mother gave them a quick signal to say nothing.

Three or four plastic stacking chairs were brought from somewhere behind the hut—apparently this was not the chief's house but a forecourt for receiving strangers. July and Daniel straightened up with casual ease; and everyone sat down in a row or squatted in line. In order to look at whoever was speaking it was necessary to lean forward and peer along the row. Some women with tins of water on their heads had stopped a few yards off and were an audience which the chief's assembly faced, but the women did not dare come closer.

The screws that attached the sheeny mother-of-pearl plastic seat to its frame were loose on Bam's chair and his thumb worked automatically to tighten them as he listened without understanding. The chief had the sharp, impatient, sceptical voice of a man quicker than the people he keeps around him, but knew no white man's language. Why should he? It was not for him to work as a servant or go down the mines. He twitted with questions he didn't expect answered—he would look along at his men, at July, with the cocked grin of one who rejects feeble comment in advance. He bit on a match in the corner of his mouth while others talked.

July was translating, god help us. It was all gone through again. Where had they come from? Why here? —The chief he say, he ask, yes, I'm work for you, but he never see a white man he come to his boy's place.— July had taken on the inattentive face of the interpreter, arranging words without meaning for or application to himself. Daniel tittered like a flirtatious girl. Maureen laughed, too, directly to the chief; apparently it was the right thing to do, he took it as applause, his mulberry-dark wrinkled lips open, his yellowed eyes acknowledging. Then there was a turn to serious, impersonal matters; no different here from anywhere else, the rituals of power. Whether it is an audience with the Pope, an interrogation by the secret police, an interview (student days) with the dean of the faculty of architecture, after you have been presumed to have been put at ease and before you are given the unknown decision you have come for, there is the stage of the man-to-man discussion. The chief wants to know exactly what it is that's happening there, Jewburg. (The contraction is not antisemitic, it's a matter of pronunciation.) He means he wants to hear—from an eye-witness—white—what it is that has taken place at last, after three-hundred-and-fifty years, between black people and white people.

—Who is it who is blowing up the government in Pretoria? It's those people from Soweto?—

—Not only Soweto. Everywhere. Everyone is in it this time. Explain to him—there's fighting in all the towns.—

—He's know. And he's ask you, why the police doesn't arrest those people like in 1976. Like in '80. Why the police doesn't shoot.—

—The blacks in the police have joined the fighting. They won't arrest their own people any more. That was the beginning.—

—And the white soldiers, they don't shoot those police?— The chief listened to the translation of his own question, his head turned half-away, face drawn together, not prepared to be taken in by anyone.

—It's a war. It's not like that, any more... The blacks have also got guns. Bombs (miming the throwing of a hand grenade). All kinds of things. Same as the white army, every-thing that kills. People have come back from Botswana and Zimbabwe, Zambia and Namibia, from Moçambique, with guns.—

Sometimes the chief took up explication in their own lang-uage, with his men; the white man was dropped from the discussion. Maureen's concentration jerked a rein on July. —What's he say?—

—He's say he can't believe that; white people are not shooting, the government is not killing those men? Always the white men got those guns, those tanks, aeroplanes. Long time. Even from fourteen–eighteen, King George war. Even from Smuts and Vorster time. The white men can't run away. No. Why they run away?—

Us and them. Who is us, now, and who them? —They're shooting all right. But they're not the only ones with guns, now. Even planes. The blacks have Cubans flying from Moçambique and Namibia.—

Us and them. What he's really asking about: an explosion of roles, that's what the blowing up of the Union Buildings and the burning of master bedrooms is.

—And they want to kill you.— The chief spoke in English without any explanation and with a face that stopped short any show of surprise.

She—Maureen—seemed to take it she was the one ad-dressed. On the stroke of dead silence, she laughed again, to him. Perhaps she couldn't speak. And blood rose to the burned and freckled surface of her skin, the thin face glisten-ing perpetually with sweat; poor thing, she changed nakedly like a chameleon before them—something beyond her con-trol.

He—Bam—if they wanted to gloat at *umlungu*, white baas, *nkosi, morema, hosi* and his family delivered into their hands—there was nothing he would say to them. Even July did not look at the face of the one he used to insist on calling master. An exhibit has no claims on anyone. *And they want to kill you.* If it amused, if it shocked the chief—take the remark how you liked—it was his privilege, irascible, ill-nourished old man, king of migrant workers, of a wilderness of neglect, villages without men, fields without tractors, children coughing in rags. But when the edict came, *Out, get out,* that same kingly authority would have to order July to give back the vehicle; would a subject who had lived so long in the suburbs, under another authority that he had now seen destroyed (even white women looted medicine from shops), recognize a chief's order?

One or two people got up and left; perhaps the audience was over. But it was merely a lull. The chief sucked loudly and sharply through the gaps in his teeth. Everyone listened to the sound as if it were intelligible. When he spoke again it was in his own language; July translated. —You think they can find this place with those people?—

—I don't understand the chief.—

—Those people they're fighting with the others.—

July was prompted by Daniel, in their language from which one foreign word dropped out: Cubas.

—You mean will the Cubans come here? How can I say?—

—He says, the government tell him long time, the Russias and those—what Daniel speak—they going to take his country here from him.—

—Oh the government. What they said. The sort of thing they told the homeland leaders, the chiefs. But now it's black people who are making this war to get everybody's land back from the whites who took it—

—He's ask, your land too?—

—I didn't ever have any land, I don't own farms—

—Your house, too?—

—Oh my house...yes, the land only whites could build on in town—maybe they'll take that. Maybe not.—

It might be standing empty; it might be burned down. But July's woman Ellen might have moved back into his quarters in the yard and be quietly caretaking...

The chief spoke for himself again, in English. —Those people from Soweto. They come here with Russias, those other ones from Moçambique, they all want take this country of my nation. Eh? They not our nation. AmaZulu, amaXhosa, baSotho... I don't know. They were already there by the mine, coming near here. If they coming, the government it's going give me guns. Yes! They give us guns, we going kill those people when they come with their guns.— He leaned far forward, breaking the angle of his legs at the bony knees like a penknife snapped half-shut. He could have been offering the privilege of a woman to the white man: —You bring your gun and you teach how it's shooting. Before, the white people are not letting us buy gun. Even me, I'm the chief, even my father and his father's father—you know?—we not having guns. When those Soweto and Russias, what-you-call-it come, you shoot with us. You help us.— The speech broke out into the eloquence of their own language; he harangued them all, his force flew rhetoric that ended majestically with reverberations from his iron-dark, iron-spare chest showing through a cheap nylon shirt, and in the dying away of hissing breaths with a final sound like a high-note clap! at the back of his throat.

—My gun.— Bamford Smales got on his feet, turned to his wife where she sat with her two fists on her thighs. All that met him was the movement of her eyeballs under thin membranes of her lowered lids; the eyes staring at the stamped earth with the reflex shift of focus brought about by a trail of ants in her line of vision, crowding round the feeding-trough formed by the body of a crushed insect.

There was about her the aura of someone under hypnosis whom it is dangerous to touch with reality.

—My gun?—

He did not know he had lifted his arms wide until he saw July, the black men—all of them were looking at his palms open to them, sinking. —You're not going to shoot your own people. You wouldn't kill blacks. Mandela's people, Sobukwe's people.— (Would they have forgotten Luthuli? heard of Biko? Not of their 'nation' although he was famous in New York and Stockholm, Paris, London and Moscow.) —You're not going to take guns and help the white government kill blacks, are you? Are you? For this—this village and this empty bush? And they'll kill you. You mustn't let the government make you kill each other. The whole black nation is your nation.—

Like the chief, like July, like everyone, she was hearing him say what he and she had always said, it came lamenting, searching from their whole life across the silent bush in which they had fallen from the fabric of that life as loose buttons drop and are lost.

The match worked from the right corner of the chief's mouth to the left. He sucked once at the gap in his teeth. —How many you got there by Mwawate's place?— One eye closed, hands in position, taking aim. Of course, 'July' was a name for whites to use; for fifteen years they had not been told what the chief's subject really was called.

—It's a shot-gun, to kill birds. Birds to eat. Oh and I did get two wart-hogs with it.—

—You not got another kind, revolver?— The kind white men are known to keep in their bedrooms, to protect their radios and TV sets and coveted suits of clothing.

—I don't shoot people.—

A short disgusted snort from the black man; a backwash of laughter.

And when you are disbelieved you begin somehow to accommodate, to fit the accusation: not to believe yourself. The parrot-call of the whites back there had been 'You mean to say you wouldn't defend your own wife and children?' Her husband kicked the big dead insect from before her, the thing landed among and sent squealing Gina and the threesome made with black children out in the heat. The child ran off clutched intimately in the thrilled group, and he had to call after her, she would disappear into the dark of this hut or that and wouldn't be found, as usual, taken in, by those who lived inside, as neither he nor his wife ever were; beer-drink familiarity was of the order of pub acquaintance between men who never invited each other to their houses. —We're leaving now, time to go!—

—Aw no...not yet... Going home?—

Yes, home. Gina was at home among the chickens, hearth ashes and communal mealie-meal pots of July's place. Bamford Smales and his wife and the chief were together a few minutes longer, standing about now, smiling, exchanging remarks about the need for rain again; thanks, and protestations of pleasure at meeting. The chief implied that he was open to complaints about July. —Everything it's all right there. He's doing nice, you getting food, what you want?—

It was she who smiled at July, said what had to be said. —We owe him everything.—

The two white people stepped forward, one by one, to shake the chief's hand and those of his elders. He parted from the white man as if acknowledging an invitation. —I come to see that gun. You teach me.—

In the vehicle they did not speak in front of July. It was July himself who challenged criticism, or merely explained (Maureen might be able to interpret his attitude, Bam not). —The African people is funny people. They don't want know this nation or this nation. The country people. Only his own nation we know, each one.—

Maureen seemed to follow. —Your chief wants to be left alone. But it's not possible.—

—He's talking talking. Talking too much.—

Their cautious lack of response roused a kind of obstinacy in July. —You can tell me, what he can do? You tell me?—

—He told you. He'll fight.—

—How he can fight? Did you see him fight when the government is coming, telling him he must pay tax? When they saying he must kill some his cattle? He must do this or this. He is our chief, but he doesn't fight when the white people tell him he must do what they want—*they* want. Now how can he fight when the black soldiers come, they say do this or this. How can he fight? He is poor man. He is chief but poor man, he hasn't got money. If they come over here, those what-you-call-it, the people from Soweto they bring them, they eat his mealies, they hungry, kill a cow—what he's going do? Can't do nothing. Talking, talking.—

The heat of their three bodies welded them together on the seat. July was driving; he took them right up almost to the door of the hut, his mother's house that he had given them, they drew apart from one another as the wet flesh of a ripe fruit gives. Then he drove away to put the yellow bakkie in its hiding-place taking Victor, Gina and Royce along for the ride, picking up other children who ran after him as he went, part of the same gang. Daniel sat up front, he and July were side by side again. When they walked to the settlement July would have the keys of the vehicle back in his pocket.

It was the first time the Smales had had to come home to: the iron bed, the Primus, the pink glass cups and saucers in the enamel basin with its sores of rust, the tin of milk powder and the general-store packet of sugar covered with a newspaper. Living within the hut they had lost sense of it. But now it was waiting for them. Coming from the stare of the sun into the dim enclosure smelled rather than seen—old, smoky grass and earth damp with what spilled from vessels and human bodies instead of dew and rain—they scarcely made each other out. In a tin-bright angle of sunlight drawn by the slide-rule of the doorway a fowl with a bald neck was sitting on the suitcase of their possessions. Maureen read the labels to herself as if she had never seen them before. Statler-Hilton Buenos Aires   Albergo San Lorenzo Mantua Heerengracht Hotel Cape Town. Bam chased the fowl.

—Don't lie on the bed.—

They could see each other now, blotched by dazzle. He

turned only to give her a look: who says I was going to. She lit the Primus; it was the oily smell of home. They had had a friend, once detained on suspicion of working with blacks for this revolution, who burned the sweaters she had worn in prison because she couldn't dissociate from the wool the smell of the cell in which they'd warmed her.

He turned the tuning knob of the radio and tried the aerial at every angle its swivel allowed. His fingers moved in hesitant concentration, someone feeling out, listening for the combination that would spring a lock. The aerial wavered the single antenna of an injured crayfish he had once caught at Gansbaai. She attracted his attention with a new battery held up, end to end, between thumb and forefinger. He shook his head. There is no music of the spheres, science killed that along with all other myths; there are only the sounds of chaos, roaring, rending, crackling out of which the order that is the world has been won. No peace beyond this world—not there, either. When the racket was lost a moment, only a cosmic sigh; they heard the sough of time and space, the wave poised over everything.

—Let me have a go.—

—Magic touch...— Their black box was ceded to her; but this one would not contain the record of their disaster, their crash from the suburb to the wilderness. It would only bring to them the last news, before silence, from Military Area Radio Network. Perhaps that had come already. She tried everything he had tried, and then twirled wildly. —Bloody thing.— Handed it back; he hung it on the nail where the previous occupant of the hut had hung her hoe.

In place of chaos, the sounds of July's—the chief's—form of order came to them. Someone droning song in rhythm with movement. The hiccuping wail of a baby being joggled on someone's back, old voices and young shouts in the concourse that was to these people newspaper, library, archives and theatre. And from over there, always to be heard, near and far, beyond where she could still see the yellow of the bakkie under black twigs, the sound of water gouting slowly from the narrow neck of a jar—the cuckoo falcon that called, beckoned and never showed itself in the bush that had no other side.

—If only I could have heard better. Even in Portuguese I might have been able to make out if—

Her expectant face, put on to dismiss rather than express any confidence: his mouth open to speak drew in air instead, he stroked roughly from under his chin down his throat as if he couldn't breathe.

—What was the wave-length? Did you remember? You're sure?—

—You tried every wave-length yourself.—

—Perhaps it's the set. We can borrow Daniel's when they come back. The bakkie's there; I don't know where they've got to, I don't see them.— She no longer had to worry about her children; she fed them; they knew how to look after themselves, like the black children.

He lingered about in the small space of the hut behind her, she could hear him hitting his fist into his palm as he did back there when he was talking about some building project he was hoping to be commissioned to design. Impossible to imagine what was happening in those suburban malls now, where white families ate ice-cream together on Saturday morning shopping trips, bought T-shirts stamped with their names ('Victor' 'Gina' 'Royce'), and looked, learning about foreign parts, at photographic exhibitions whose favoured subject was black township life.

—There was that report last year—I don't know any more, probably several years ago—United States Congress was told by their Research Service it was possible U.S. aircraft would be sent in to rescue American citizens if they were in danger.

And it was mentioned—don't you remember?—in the news the first week after we got here, I was putting up the tank... It just could be that what we heard—

—You heard, I didn't.—

—...it just could be what that was. Pretoria, Johannesburg, United States Congress...—

She was pressing back the cuticles grown like dry cobwebs up her earth-rimmed toenails. Squatted in the doorway; Maureen who had been so at ease in her body, a dancer's repose even if she wasn't much as a dancer, examined herself with the obsessive attention of the confined, left to nothing but themselves. —Aircraft to rescue *Americans*.—

—And citizens of other European nations. I remember distinctly. A man called Robson, it was his report to Congress. No, not Robson, Copson—that's it.—

It was not necessary for her to remind him they and their children were not Americans, or Europeans of other European nations. It was not necessary for him to remind her that they *could have been* Europeans of Canadian citizenship. If all whites became the same enemies, to blacks, all whites might become 'Europeans' for the Americans?

She felt his eyes upon her hands picking at her toes. She stretched her legs and tucked the hands out of the way under her armpits. —What about the business of the gun?—

He came and squatted. His mouth worked half-smilingly before he spoke. —You know what I thought. I thought it was going to be something else. He was going to tell us to push off.— Anything a relief so long as it was not going to be that.

Her head turned away.

She spoke from there. —What about the gun?—

—Can you see me as a mercenary.—

Her inner gaze was directed by him, at himself. She had been asked to note someone who had just arrived, but she saw the man who had been left behind.

—Throwing South African army hand-grenades to protect some reactionary poor devil of a petty chief against the liberation of his own people.—

She took her hands from under her arms and they clapped listlessly together: oh all that. The phrases they had used back there.

—Wha'd'you think I am.— Anger began to turn in him a wheel that would not engage.

—What'll you do if he does come. If he walks over for his lesson in marksmanship.—

—What rubbish. One shot-gun. A toy—this is bush warfare.—

—He thinks of it only as a sample, a demonstration model. There'll be other weapons—as you said, South African hand-grenades. The last handout from the government to their homeland chiefs. So if he comes...—

Pragmatism, that's all, she had said when they first arrived in this dump and she had reproached herself for learning ballet dancing instead of—at least—the despised *Fanagalo*. And he had said, of back there, if it's been lies, it's been lies. He struggled hopelessly for words that were not phrases from back there, words that would make the truth that must be forming here, out of the blacks, out of themselves. He sensed for a moment the great drama hidden in the monotonous days, as she was aware, always, of the yellow bakkie hidden in the sameness of bush. But the words would not come. They were blocked by an old vocabulary, 'rural backwardness', 'counter-revolutionary pockets', 'failure to bring about peaceful change inevitably leading to civil war'—she knew all that, she had heard all that before it happened. And now it had happened, it was an experience that couldn't be forethought. Not with the means they had satisfied themselves with. The words were not there; his mind, his anger, had no grip. —You saw he 'let me' drive, going there?... A treat for me. July's pretty sure of himself these days. He doesn't seem to think much of his chief, anyway. You heard the way he talked.—

She blinked slowly two or three times. —I think July was talking about himself.—

—Himself? How?— Now she was actually saying something, not provoking him to give himself away in some manner he didn't understand; he didn't want either to slip the frail noose or tighten it on himself by the wrong reaction.

—*He* always did what whites told him. The pass office. The police. Us. How will he not do what blacks tell him, even if he has to kill his cows to feed the freedom fighters.—

—But it will come better from them.— (Some of the old phrases were real.) —For his own people. Even if they do need the help of the Cubans and Russians to bring it about.—

—So July won't fight any Holy Wars for that old man. He didn't murder us in our beds and he won't be a warrior for his tribe, either.—

—Oh murder us in our beds!— Moving after her along this track and that, losing her. —You don't think (he stopped) you're not thinking he was a sell-out to bring us here—are you? Not that?—

—What do the blacks think? What will the freedom fighters think? Did he join the people from Soweto? He took his whites and ran. You make me laugh. You talk as if we weren't hiding, we weren't scared to go farther than the river?—

—Of course we're hiding. From (his neck stiffened, his head shuddered frustration rather than shook denial)— from...temporary rage and senseless death. *He's* hiding us.—

—He's been mixed up with us for fifteen years. No one will ever be able to disentangle that, so long as he's alive; is that it? A fine answer to give the blacks who are getting killed to set him free.—

—Good god! He runs the risk of getting killed himself,

for having us here! Although I don't think he realizes, luckily...—
—Then we'd better go.—
She was looking at him as he had never seen her before, with dead eyes, triumphantly, as if he had killed her himself, expecting nothing of him. —So we'd better go, then. *You* can't be a mercenary. *He* didn't join his own people in town.—
The two of them were regarding—he himself was conscious of—a heavy blond man, his reddened skull wrinkled with anguish above angry eyes. —Where? Where?—
At the same instant both heard (again, strangely, the couple in the master bedroom about to be burst in upon while making love on Sunday morning) the approaching voices of their children.
But she would not let him avoid the logical conclusion of his question. She was telling him as Royce raced up, prancing, tripping and shadow-boxing one of his own heroic fantasies of adult life: —How. And how?—

The white woman did not understand they were going to cut grass, not gather leaves for boiling. She followed, and pointed at the old woman's sickle, silver-black, slick as a snake's tongue, with cowhide thongs woven round the hand-piece. It had been taken down from the dark of the special hut where the wooden yoke and chains for the plough-oxen were kept. Martha had her one-year-old hump of baby on her back and on her head an enamel basin with a small machete, cold *pap* tied in a cloth, and an old orange-squash bottle filled with a pale mixture of water, powdered milk and tea. She shaped for the white woman the few Afrikaans words she could find; these included a slang catch-all brought back from the mines and cities by men of the village who were the gang labourers of poorly-educated white foremen: *Dingus*, thing, whatsisname. —*Vir die huis. Daardie dingus.*— Her hands were free, her head steady under its heavy crown, she lifted elbows and sketched the pitch of a roof. The old woman half-closed her faded eyes and growled low and friendly affirmation. While her daughter-in-law tried to satisfy the questions of this white woman who had had to be taught the difference between a plant that even a cow knew better than to chew, and the leaves that would make her children strong, the old woman had the chance to look at her closely in the satisfying, analytical way she didn't often get without the woman disguising herself by trying, with her smiles and gestures, to convey respect etc. as she thought this was done by black people. July had told his mother again and again, the white woman was different at home. He meant that place that had a white china room to do your business in, even he had one in the yard. She had never worked for whites—only in weeding parties on their farms, and there in the lands they didn't tell her where to go and do it. She wouldn't be told that by whites!

The grass was the correct height, the weather neither too damp nor too hot and dry—exactly right for cutting thatching grass, and she, who knew the best sources for all the materials she used for her brooms and her roofs, was on her way to a stretch up-river she had been watching for weeks. Since before her son brought his white people. She grinned with top lip pursed rubbery down over her empty gums and pointed a first finger as if to prod the white woman in the chest: You, yes you.

But the white woman didn't understand she meant the grass was to thatch the house the white woman had taken from her. Martha reproached her mother-in-law in their language; yet it was true; and she could say what she liked, anyway, the woman understood nothing. The poor thing, the *nhwanyana* (July's mother used the term, *my lady*, that had come down to her attached to any white female face, from the conquests of the past), the white woman was grinning back to show she had taken up the joke, whatever she imagined it was... *They have money, let them go to their relatives, to other white people, if they're in trouble*: the old woman talked as the little party went through the bush. If her daughter-in-law didn't or wouldn't listen, the words became simply a refrain.

—Now they have been there. He's greeted them.—

Several days after he had taken the white people to visit the chief, July's wife spoke to July of what she was thinking. She was not used to having him present to communicate with directly; there was always the long wait for his answering letter, a time during which she said to herself in different ways what it was she had wanted and tried to tell him in her letters. Once she sent a telegram. There had been trouble with her younger brother; fighting, and a hut burned. But the man who knew how to go to the white farm store that was also a post office said never mind, he knew what you said in telegrams, and wrote MOTHER VERY SICK COME HOME.

Now her man was in her hut, she was giving him his food, he was there to look at her when she said something. —The chief can give them a place in his village, then.—

When July didn't answer at once she couldn't wait. —Perhaps he's going to.—

Trying to hem him in with her reasoning; she thought she was chasing a chicken? —Why should the chief do that? Who told you that?—

—Nobody told me.— After a moment: —You took them there.—

—So you yourself are the one who thinks the chief will give them a house.—

—Did you ask him?—

He scooped and balled the *pap* vigorously between his fingers and ate a mouthful; lifted a graceful smeared hand to show he would have something to say in a moment, in a moment.

She could wait; perhaps he was trying to think of an answer to all the questions she might have for him, who had learned so much she did not know.

—You are the one who is asking him. Aren't you? Not me. I saw, you've put the bundles of thatching grass outside their house—all right, *mhani*'s house, I know. But why did you do that?— He added what both knew was not the reason for his objection. —Their children are playing with it. It will all be broken and spoiled. You'll waste your work.—

—*She* said it was time. The grass was right. She wanted to cut before the other women took the best. I can't tell your mother she mustn't do what she wants. I am her daughter, I must help her. Perhaps you have also forgotten some things.—

—What do you mean?—

Her head on one side again, to ward off anger, but not afraid, her wheedling cringing force. —You have to learn all their things, such a long time. When you go.—

—More than fifteen years. Yes... The first time was in 1965. But I didn't work for them, then. I worked in that hotel, washing up in the kitchen. I had no papers, that time. All of us in the kitchen had no papers, the owner let us sleep in the store-room, he locked us in so nobody could steal and take food out.— An old story, his story; her head nodded to check each point. —That was the place that burned down, afterwards, in the winter their paraffin stove started a fire there, they couldn't get out. God was good to me.—

He had not burned to death in the white man's city, he had brought home from that job the money to pay her father (he had already paid the cattle). She had had her first child by then, and she became his wife. That was what happened to her, her story; he came home every two years and each time, after he had gone, she gave birth to another child. Next year would have been the time again, but now he had brought his white people, he had come to her after less than two years and already she had not bled this month.

He looked at her, painfully, pityingly, as if by so doing to block out seeing something or someone else. He spoke with the rush of an enthusiasm there was not time to examine. —When the fighting's over I'll take you with me, I'll take you back and show you, you'll stay there with me. And the children too.—

Her chin thrust forward, mouth jaunty, eyes sliding to the corners of her lids, she seemed to be discovering herself in the eyes of other people. —Me, there! What would I do in those places.— Gasping and making scornful, tender clicks in her throat. —Can you see me in their yard! How would I know my road, who would tell me where to go?— She laughed and shivered bashfully. She made to take the food away but he put out his hand to show he was not finished, although he didn't eat, again seeing something she could not know about; those Ndebele women who came in from the veld north of the city and crossed the streets bewilderedly under backward glances and giggles, their tall vase-shaped headdresses of clay-and-hair covered by striped hand-towels, old canvas football boots on their feet below cylinders of brass-wire anklets.

Laughter, the bashfulness sank slowly from the settling muscles of her face, and the baby boy, loosed from the pouch on her back, pulled at the objects that were her nose, her lips, her small black ears and the tight string of dirt-etched blue beads, prescribed by a tribal doctor, she was always armed with against misfortune. —After the fighting is over, perhaps you can stay here. You said the job was finished. If we get more lands and we grow more mealies...a tractor to plough...

◊ *134*

Daniel says we're going to get these things. We won't have to pay tax to the government. Daniel says. You wouldn't have to pay the whites for a licence, you could have a shop here, sell soap and matches, sugar—you know how to do it, you've seen the shops in town. You understand as well as the India how to buy things and bring them from town. And now you can drive. For yourself. I see those men of our people who drive big lorries for white men. But you drive for yourself.—

The vehicle that had brought his white people had never been mentioned between the two of them. She had not remarked upon or praised his prowess while he was learning to drive it. He had said nothing; it was natural for him to assume she saw him serving his white people in this way just as he took them wood and had given them his mother's house and the pink glass cups and saucers.

There was complicity growing in the silence. He broke it. —After the fighting... If you could have seen how it was in town. I was there. You die just like that.— There were thoughts that had to be tried out on someone. —I left my money. I couldn't fetch it, anyway. Everything was closed up. Finished.—

In the shoulder-bag AEROLINEAS ARGENTINAS his white man had passed on after the return from the architects' congress in Buenos Aires he kept the simulated-calf wallet they had given him one Christmas. It was flattened and softened to its contents by the years he had carried it always against the contours of the body in hip or breast pocket; his passbook that his employers had to sign every month, his post office savings book, the building society savings book with its initial deposit entry of one hundred rands they had given him in recognition of ten years' service, five years ago. The figures in his post office book rose and fell, from three figures sometimes to one. He put in five rands of Fah-Fee winnings when he was very, very lucky, he took out sums to send home when there was a crisis in his family, far from his intervention—the only authority left to him, at that distance, was money. He withdrew the savings of two years' work, his entire capital, all he was worth to the city he was spending his life in, all that there ever was between him and a slump, unemployment, sudden disaster, old age and destitution, each time he went home on leave. He never had withdrawn anything from the United Building Society account with the hundred rands, and it had grown by itself, a rand or two a year: they explained interest to him, how money could be earned without working for it, the system whites had invented for themselves. He had never seen the money they gave him, or touched it, but it was there. They had saved him, when first he came to them, from his country ignorance, keeping his money in a cigarette tin under his mattress.

—How much?— She knew what his monthly wage was, and didn't tell anyone else because people always ask to borrow. But she didn't understand the source of other odd sums that came his way and sometimes were passed on to her and his mother—not always, she saw that when he used to come home on the railway bus in new clothes; this last time, two years ago, in blue jeans and matching zip-up jacket. She did not know what other money there was to be gained, or how, and on whom he spent it. The gambling game was not one that was played here at his home. A backyard, back-lanes game where the money rolled from white houses.

They had told him his money was safe, written down in those books. But now that they had run away, those books were just bits of paper. Like the other things he and his wife and his mother and all the people here kept in the dark of huts because there was so little left over from the needs of each day: the safety medal someone brought back from the mines, the Mickey Mouse watch Victor had ruined in the

bath, the receipt for the bicycle paid for six hundred kilometres away.

He made a rough equivalent for her. —More than a
hundred pounds.— The people here at home had never
changed their calculation to the currency of rands and cents,
the Indian store still marked in the old British currency the
price of Primus stoves and zinc finials which, for those who
could afford them, had replaced the cone of mud packed on
the apex of roofs to secure the highest layer of thatch.

He thought of the pass-book itself as finished. Rid of it, he
drove the yellow bakkie with nothing in his pockets. But he
had not actually destroyed it. He needed someone—he didn't
yet know who—to tell him: burn it, let it swell in the river,
their signatures washing away.

A man in short trousers came along the valley carrying a red box on his head. She was watching him all the way; she could no longer stay in the hut while the blond man fiddled with the radio. The children had stood obstinately before her, squinting into the sun through wild hair, when she forbade them to go swimming in the river, and she could hear their squeals as they jumped like frogs from boulder to boulder in the brown water with children who belonged here, whose bodies were immune to water-borne diseases whose names no one here knew. Maybe the three had become immune, too. They had survived in their own ability to ignore the precautions it was impossible for her to maintain for them. Victor was forgetting how to read, but did not miss his Superman and Asterix; she sat outside the hut and could not understand *I Promessi Sposi*. It was translated from the Italian but would not translate from the page to the kind of comprehension she was able to provide now. Only the account of bread riots in Milan in 1628 produced in her, in reflex, an olfactory impression of bread, and even that was not a craving for bread (there was none here, mealie-meal *pap* was bread), for the supply from the supermarket that was always ready, wrapped in plastic bags, in the freezer back there—was not a real connection made between her normal sense of self and her present circumstances, but simply the statement of the bread Lydia baked once a week. In the kitchen of the Married Quarters house on the mine, along the passage—as you opened the door, the house bloomed with the slightly fermented scent. And it was Lydia's heavy brown bread in brick-shaped loaves. Rather tasteless; it had given all in what it breathed through the house.

She was not in possession of any part of her life. One or another could only be turned up, by hazard. The background had fallen away; since that first morning she had become conscious in the hut, she had regained no established point of a continuing present from which to recognize her own sequence. The suburb did not come before or after the mine. 20, Married Quarters, Western Areas, and the architect-designed master bedroom were in the same rubble. A brick picked up might be Lydia's loaf.

The red box on the man's head showed first under the bold black-green of the wild fig-trees at the river. A bit of red leaped out at her; no one knew from which direction anyone might have come, in the homogeneity of the bush out there, she watched it all day and saw nothing, it absorbed, concealed what it held. If people came from the other side of the river they appeared for the first time, broken up by foliage and flashes off the water they disturbed as they crossed the river; and as they rearranged their bundles and their clothes after wading through with these on their heads. But this was some sort of trunk or box, bright red. It appeared now as red splinters between the elephant grass on the near side of the river. The man climbed the gradient towards her—not seeing her, there were bushes, there was a great pile of thatch someone had dumped, she felt she was not there—with bowed black shins staggering. The trousers were not shorts but had worn through and been torn off at the knees. The red box was heavy and there were wires looped from it that bothered him. He hailed once, towards the huts. Having announced himself, plodded on. A fix on him, she had felt the bunching of muscles in his neck as he braced himself against rising ground under the red box, the cold tingling in the arm from which the blood receded where it was raised to steady the box; the sweat of his effort melting in the heat of the day was the sweat of her hands' imprint wetting the pages of the book. He was lost to her behind Martha's chicken-house on stilts and the water-tank when he reached the village.

In the afternoon there was a deafening, fading and lurching bellow through the air; it was the *gumba-gumba* being tried out, the children reported.

Here was something for which Victor, Gina and Royce knew the name in the village people's language but not in their own. The red box was the area's equivalent of a travelling entertainment; someone had brought back from the mines a battery-operated amplifier and apparently he would come and set it up in this village or that, attached to a record player, for an occasion. It was not clear what this occasion was. Mother and father were tugged along by the Smales children to see the *gumba-gumba*, which the children couldn't believe was not something unknown to them. —How can you say what it's like?— For Gina, what hadn't before been seen in this village was new to the world.

The parents were brought together to witness the contraption as divorced people might meet on their regular day to keep up a semblance of family life. They exchanged a few words with July, another parent, his second youngest sitting yoked on his shoulders. He had the city man's good-natured amusement at country people's diversions. Bam asked whether there was a wedding? And added, or a meeting? But July was not apart from the leisurely, straggling group coming and going about the focus of the man who had commandeered a couple of youths to help him rig up his wires and speaker horn on one of the wattle poles of the hut that was also some kind of church or meeting-house—often women's voices singing hymns came from there. —Is not a wedding.— And at the idea of a meeting, he merely laughed. —Sometime we having a party. Just because someone he's... I don't know. I don't know what it is.— He called up to the man on the roof in the way his people did, teasing and encouraging, the first part of what he said gabbled and rapid, the syllables of the last word strongly divided and drawn out, the word itself repeated. *Mi ta twa ku nandziha ngopfu, swi famba a moyeni. Ncino wa maguva lawa, hey—i... hey—i!*

Laughter and comment flew from people come out of their huts and flocked up around the man and July. The *gumba-gumba* was itself the occasion; the dropsical man (whose legs lately were bandaged in rags of a filthy towel), sometimes the presence of a beggar, today—because of the voice of the oracle yelling and retching from its battered red box and dented horn—sat on his stool as an old god carried out among them, the grotesque ceremonial presence without which carnival forgets its origin is in fear of death. Music began swirling unsteadily from the amplifier. Already they were passing round the thin beer that was the same colour when drunk and when vomited. Their fun had its place in their poverty. It ignored that they were in the middle of a war, as if poverty itself were a country whose dispossession nothing reaches.

July's white people wandered away. The father did not want to have to drink that stuff and did not want to offend.

The mother thought there were pleasanter sights for the children than—in particular—some of the women (not July's, ever) getting drunk with their babies on their backs, and going to pee only as far away as their staggering would carry them.

When the white family got back to the hut the gun was gone.

If he hadn't been with them watching the installation of the *gumba-gumba* they would have thought it was Victor. Quite possible he would boast that he was allowed to handle his father's gun; would have somehow climbed up and taken it from its place in the roof.

The boxes of cartridges had gone, too.

Bam was just as he was when the car keys were lost back there. But his hands shook, actually shook—she saw it as she had often pretended not to know when someone was crying. There were so few places to search, in a hut, and where could the gun be, if it were not in its place and had not been moved by him? Who would move it?

He seemed suddenly unsure he might not have moved it himself. After coming back from the chief. She had always been asked to check whether her passport was really in her travel wallet, when they travelled together. She had done this with exaggerated precision, holding it up to him in her way between thumb and first finger, putting it back where it had been and she had been sure it had been, all the time.

She looked under the coverings they used as bed-clothes and pitched their few crumpled clothes out of the suitcase.

He even took the knob-kerrie he had been given by an old man in exchange for fish and poked in the thatch that was piled up outside, lifted the bundles one by one and flung them aside. Victor and Royce rummaged, talking too much. —What if someone's buried it? C'mon, let's dig, Vic? Shall we dig?— When checked in one activity, they dashed to another. They forgot what they were supposed to be searching for; turning over ashes became a contest of kicking the grey powder at one another. Gina had run off to skip with Nyiko, who had an old dressing-gown cord for a rope.

—You're quite sure you didn't play with it? At *any* time?—

—No, daddy—man! I promise.— Victor was offended at being suspected of what he knew he might very well have done.

The younger one indemnified, innocent of everything, for all time: —We never. Cross my heart.—

—Because no one else knew it was there.— Their father's look held. He breathed as if he had been running; even as they did when they were about to cry.

The boys stood waiting for whatever it was grown-ups might decide to do. Neither would dare risk telling their father everybody knew it was there, every chicken that scratched, every child whose eyes went round the interior of the hut, *mhani* Tsatsawani's hut, where the white people stayed. —*Gina* knows.— Royce told tales, but the father didn't understand the implication. And Victor, his hand out of sight where he stood close up beside his young brother, took the flap of the little boy's skinny thigh and pinched it

with steadily maintained pressure for a few seconds, enforc-
ing a code of loyalty that extended even to their sister in time
of real trouble.

—You c'n tell the police, dad.—

Bam looked behind, around him; sat down on the bed. He
nodded a long time.

She saw that he wouldn't answer the child; but he was
back there: if he couldn't pick up the phone and call the police whom he and she had despised for their brutality and
thuggery in the life lived back there, he did not know what
else to do.

He heaved himself up. Some surge of adrenalin summoned,
sending him striding out, ducking his big head under the
doorway. But he walked immediately into their gaze again.
He lay down on his back, on that bed, the way he habitually
did; and at once suddenly rolled over onto his face, as the
father had never done before his sons.

They looked to their mother but her expression was closed
to them. Even her body—so familiar in the jeans as worn as
the covering of a shabby stuffed toy, the T-shirt stretched
over the flat small breasts that were soft to lie against—they
knew, as they had learnt when a dog or cat was going to
repulse them, that to touch was forbidden them.

She looked down on this man who had nothing, now.
There was before these children something much worse than
the sight of the women's broad backsides, squatting.

The moon in the sky was a circle of gauze pasted up on the
afternoon blue. Maureen Smales—the name, the authority
that signed his pass every month—came back to the *gumba-
gumba* gathering to look for July. For Mwawate. He was not
there; they were used to her, they took no more notice of her
than of the dogs and children who hung around the drinkers'

mysterious animation, quarrelsome happiness and resentful sadness.

She went to his hut—not his private quarters, but the home of his women. Martha was bathing the baby boy in a basin set on a box. Flashing tears of pure anger he appealed to the one—anyone—who had arrived to rescue him from soap and water. These black women were tranquil through their children's tantrums; Martha did not seem to hear the screams and considering a moment, looking no higher than at the white woman's feet, in servility, as if they had not walked and worked in the fields together, indicated she didn't know where July was. Somewhere about. His mother sat under her skirts beside the hearth ashes. When she was not actively working she was very old and still; she leaned with a twig in her hand and blew a faint glow in the grey as if it were her own life she was keeping just alight.

There was a moment when Maureen could have got on her hunkers beside Martha and helped hold the baby's head while its hair was washed.

Martha asked her nothing; July had to do what he was told by this woman when he worked in town, she claimed the right to know where he was, even here at his home.

She couldn't tell Martha why she wanted July; it was not a matter of language, they had communicated before. She couldn't tell Martha what she herself felt herself to be, what had happened to her. She saw Martha securely petrified, madonna drawing snuff into one nostril above a baby's head, *pietà* with a machine-gunned son across her lap. Martha had laughed at veined white legs. At one time (the longings of Maureen Smales from back there) it seemed a beginning. Something might have come of it. But not much.

She left the women and their hearth and jogged down into the grass below the village. The habit of the pace came from spare-time attention given to many things, back there: your health, your sense of injustice done, your realization of living a life that was already over—these were the dutiful half-hour recognitions that did not affect normal daily abuse. When the Smales couple ran round the suburban blocks under the jacarandas they didn't know what they were running from. She was following in reverse, as if with a finger on a map, the way the *gumba-gumba* man had come towards her. The grass shushed past her knees, her passage scything it folded back on either side. Orange-polka-dotted black beetles that weighed the stalks were transferred from their feeding-ground to her bare calves and her clothes. Rough seeds burred together the rolled-up legs of her jeans. The vegetation fingered and touched; there were minute ticks that waited a whole season for the passing of an animal or human host. That was the intimate nature of the inert bush dissolving distance.

She did not expect to find him at the river but it was where the invisible route traced by the red box was taking her. She had not gone often to the river except on very private errands, and then not to the place where the children swam, where it was forded. Even here, when there was nobody, there was little sign that there was ever anybody. The people had nothing superfluous with which to litter; the shallows sank into the depressions made in mud by their feet and mingled them with the kneading of cattle hooves. Muslin scraps of butterflies settled on turds. She could name the variety of thorn-tree—*Dichrostachys cinerea, sekelbos*—with its yellow tassels dangling from downy pink and mauve pom-poms, both colours appearing on the same branch. Roberts' bird book and standard works on indigenous trees and shrubs were the Smales' accommodation of the wilderness to themselves when they used to visit places like this, camping out. At the end of the holiday you packed up and went back to town.

There was the stillness of unregarded trees and ceaseless water. On the huge pale trunks wild figs bristled like bunches of hat-pins. The earth was sour with fallen fruit; between the giant trees a tan fly-catcher swooped, landing to hover on the invisible branches of a great tree of air. Again, she had the feeling of not being there, that she had had while the man with the red box was climbing into her vision. The slight rise and fall of her breathing produced no ripple of her counter-existence in the heavy peace. The systole and diastole needed only to cease, and she would be ingested, disappeared in this state of being that needed no witnesses. She was unrecorded in any taxonomy but that of Maureen Hetherington on her points to applause in the Mine Recreation Hall.

She withdrew, every twig a trap sprung by her weight. She took the old way to him, joining the single-file path he and Daniel had made, tending the vehicle, from the village. Their club, their retreat, meeting-place... She and Bam had talked of converting the garage into a room where July could sit with his friends, putting an old sofa there, but both knew that since he would be the only servant in the suburb with such a privilege, there would be too many friends in and out the backyard, too much noise.

She found him there sitting on one of their home-made stools at the left side of the vehicle—probably because of the shade it had cast; the sun was low enough now for that to be unnecessary. Neither cleaning nor repairing the vehicle; but the *gumba-gumba* and the beer were not for him despite his show of participation. He was writing with an old short lead pencil in a note-book, calculating something as he used to keep his gambling accounts. The note-book was one of the desk-top promotions sent by building-supply firms to architects each Christmas. It was stained with red earth and the corners had curled with handling. He saw she recognized it. It seemed they were about to exchange some reminiscence.

—You've got to get that gun back.—

He screwed up his face irritably, jerked his chest: what was this?

—The gun's gone. It was kept in the roof.—

She saw that he had not known. But he was not surprised. He sucked at his cheeks and closed the note-book with the pencil between the pages. —When someone's take it?—

—I don't know when. It wasn't there any more when we came back from going to see them put up that thing for the music.—

He accused her. —How someone's can take it?—

She flung back at him his uprightness, his moralizing—whatever the rigmarole of form he had always insisted on establishing between them. —Why not, July? Why not? Just walk into the hut when we're not there and take it. Steal it.—

—Now-now?—

—Bam discovered it now. But it might not have been this afternoon. It could have been any time.—

—When he's see it last time?—

—Doesn't seem to know himself. But it was still there when we came back from the chief's. We talked about it. I saw it.—

—You sure the gun it's there before this afternoon? Because everybody he's there at the music. You see everybody was there, hey? Nobody can come to the house that time.—

—How do I know if it was still there then? I told you. I know everyone was at the music.—

—Night-time.— He let the two of them visualize it. —Night-time, you all sleeping, you all in the house. Who can come.—

—It's not Victor.— July knew that possibility as well as anyone. —You can forget about Victor.—

—No, no, Victor he's so nice. Naughty boy sometime but so nice. And if he's take, he's show his friend, he's put back, isn't it. Not Victor. Well, everybody here so nice at the music today, everybody know that gun it's your gun—

—Where's Daniel?—

She was distracted by something misplaced. What would appear for her from beneath the vehicle, from the ruined huts, so often a silent presence while not yet noticed: now he surely would come forward to July's call with his young man's easy stroll.

—*Daniel* wasn't there— Her voice alight; at the same time, some kind of fear and amazement came like a sack thrown dark over her head. —Where's Daniel?—

—Daniel he's not come any more.— A hand lifted, at large a moment, slid under the neck of the shirt. The gauze round of moon had become opaque and polished with the light of the vanished sun; it began gently to reflect, a mirror being adjusted. The shadow of the vehicle fell upon them and reached out in its blown-up detail, roof-rack and spare tyre, over the bright, watery lacings of sunset in grass and bushes. —One, two day now he's going.—

—But you know where he is. He told you where he was going?—

He spoke of these young ones. —They not asking anyone, anyone. Not even the father.—

—But he told you, he discussed it with you, he must have talked to you. You and he are together all the time. *You* were like his father, weren't you. You can't say to me he didn't tell you?— Two gnats she had swatted against her face stuck drowned in sweat on her cheek.

—Don't tell me what Daniel he tell me. Me, I know if he's say or he's not say nothing. Is not my business, isn't it?—

She sat down on the mud wall that was warmed to life all through the heat of the day and whose colour had risen, amber, blood-purple out of terra-cotta in the thick layer of last light suspended at a man's height across the earth.

—You've got to get it back.—

She knew those widened nostrils. Go, he willed, go up the hill to the hut; as he would to his wife.

He could smell her cold cat-smell she had when she sweated. The only way to get away from her was to walk off and leave her, give up to her this place that was his own, the place he had found to hide the yellow bakkie and keep it safe.

He stuffed the note-book into his shirt-pocket torn and neatly sewn back with unmatched thread by Ellen. —How I must get that gun? Where I'm going find it? You know where is it? *You* know? Then if you know why you yourself, your husband, you don't fetch it?—

—The gun's gone, Daniel's gone. He handled it, he was allowed to fire a shot with it...Bam's nonsense. He was at the chief's listening to all that talk about guns. He fancied it for himself. Didn't he? Thinks he'll kill some meat. Or he's got a customer for it.— Her lids blinked sharply at him. —Perhaps the chief. You must know where to look for him, he's with you (a gesture towards the bakkie) every day.—

He was feeling up round his neck and over his chest under the shirt while she talked at him. The hand came out swiftly and stiff fingers tapped at the centre of his being, there on the plate with its little shining black cups of hollow where the breast-muscles joined the bone. —Me? I must know who is stealing your things? Same like always. You make too much trouble for me. Here in my home too. Daniel, the chief, my-mother-my-wife with the house. Trouble, trouble from you. I don't want it any more. You see?— His hands flung out away from himself.

—You've got to get it back.—

—No no. No no.— Hysterically smiling, repeating. —I don't know Daniel he's stealing your gun. How I'm know? You, you say you know, but me I'm not see any gun, I'm not see Daniel, Daniel he's go—well what I can do—

She was stampeded by a wild rush of need to destroy everything between them, she wanted to erase it beneath her heels
as snails broke and slithered like the shell and slime of rotten
eggs under her foot in the suburban garden. —You stole
small things. Why? I wouldn't tell you then but I tell
you now. My scissors like a bird, my old mother's knife-
grinder.—

—Always you give me those thing!—

—Oh no, I gave you... but not those.—

—I don't want your rubbish.—

—Why did you take rubbish? ...I said nothing because I
was ashamed to think you would do it.—

—You— He spread his knees and put an open hand on
each. Suddenly he began to talk at her in his own language,
his face flickering powerfully. The heavy cadences surrounded
her; the earth was fading and a thin, far radiance from the
moon was faintly pinkening parachute-silk hazes stretched
over the sky. She understood although she knew no word.
Understood everything: what he had had to be, how she had
covered up to herself for him, in order for him to be her idea
of him. But for himself—to be intelligent, honest, dignified
for *her* was nothing; his measure as a man was taken else-
where and by others. She was not his mother, his wife, his
sister, his friend, his people. He spoke in English what belonged in English: —Daniel he's go with those ones like in
town. He's join.— The verb, unqualified, did for every kind
of commitment: to a burial society, a hire purchase agreement, their thumbprints put to a labour contract for the
mines or sugar plantations. —I don't know—maybe he's
need the gun for that.— He leaned back, done with her.

—I know.— Daniel's raised fist in greeting had seemed a
matter of being fashionable, for the young milkman returned
to his backward village from town, just as dropping to the
knees before the chief was surely no more than a rural con-

vention for him and July. —I know.— 'Cubas': it was he who had supplied the identification when the chief could not name the foreigners he feared. —So he's gone to fight. Little bastard. He only took what he had a right to.—

July might not have understood the claim granted, or was not going to be obliged to speak. His familiar head, newly shaved by a villager who barbered under a tree, his broad soft mouth under the moustache, his eyes white against the dark of the face blurred by the dimness, now, of all things at the earth's level under the high light of the sky, faced her. Together in this place of ruin that was the habitation of no living being, only a piece of machinery, their words sank into the broken clay walls like spilt blood. Would be buried here. The skin of her body was creeping with an ecstatic fever of relief, splendid and despicable to her. She told him the truth, which is always disloyal. —You'll profit by the others' fighting. Steal a bakkie. You want that, now. You don't know what might have happened to Ellen. She washed your clothes and slept with you. You want the bakkie, to drive around in like a gangster, imagining yourself a *big man*, important, until you don't have any money for petrol, there isn't any petrol to buy, and it'll lie there, July, under the trees, in this place among the old huts, and it'll fall to pieces while the children play in it. Useless. Another wreck like all the others. Another bit of rubbish.—

The incredible tenderness of the evening surrounded them as if mistaking them for lovers. She lurched over and posed herself, a grotesque, against the vehicle's hood, her shrunken jeans poked at the knees, sweat-coarsened forehead touched by the moonlight, neglected hair standing out wispy and rough. The death's harpy image she made of herself meant nothing to him, who had never been to a motor show complete with provocative girls. She laughed and slapped the mudguard vulgarly, as he had done to frighten a beast out of the way. The sharp sound flew back to them from the settlement. A little homely fire, the first of those for the evening meal, began to show over there as a match flame grows cupped in a palm.

Bam was giving the children food. He dug off lumps of mealie-meal he had cooked and they took it with their fingers. They were chattering and said nothing to her when she appeared, as if they thought she had been there all the time. He did not ask her where she had been; he ate with the children, using the tin spoon to which tatters of *pap* clung. She ate nothing and went into the dark hut, finding the water-bottle by feel. In there she drank the whole bottle in a series of sucking gulps broken by long pauses, like an alcoholic who hides away to indulge secret addiction. And like the family of the addict that does not know how to deal with her, they pretended not to know, or did not know.

The *gumba-gumba* had started up again with one of the same four or five records. *Baby, baby come duze—duze—duze* in close harmony, broken by the jet of a high-voiced refrain playing above it, went out into the bush over the huts and under the haze. There were no stars. *Baby, baby, du-ze, du-ze...* If there were a roving band of freedom fighters out there, they would be able to hear it, far away, the old music of Soweto, Daveyton, Tembisa, Marabastad, the town places they had burst and spread from.

When he saw her getting into what was her bed, he made the approach of remarking that her feet were awfully dirty. She got up and from July's oil-drum kept full of river water washed them with soap supplied by July. She spoke from beyond the light of the paraffin lamp. —Was it like this for him?— It was never necessary to say 'July'; he was there in their minds, there was no one else.

She was understood: but that would be too easy an equation. A hand scratched the back fringe of blond hair, felt carefully where there was none.

She matched the remembered total dependency with this one. —Used to come to ask for everything. An aspirin. Can I use the telephone. Nothing in that house was his.—

—Well...he wasn't kept short of anything. Anything we had to give.—

—I wonder what would have become of him.—

The paraffin lamp was still burning but the blue eyes were closed. —Would have got old with us and been pensioned off.—

Daniel has the gun. Taken it for himself.

Her lips moved with the words formed but not spoken. She looked a long time at the closed eyelids.

The mists of the night left a vivid freshness that dispels the sickly ammoniacal odour of fowl droppings, the fetid cloying of old thatch, the stinks of rotting garbage—rags, the jaw-bone of a calf, scaly with big glistening flies—that collect wherever the rains have hollowed the ground between huts. Women put out the lengths of cotton they wrap themselves and their babies in. A clear strong sun sweetens the fusty cloth. It glosses the grass roofs and the mud walls change under it to golden ochre; the stuff of which these houses were made is alive. At this moment in its span, its seasons, the village coincides with the generic moment of the photographer's village, seen from afar, its circles encircled by the landscape, held in the pantheistic hand, the single community of man-and-nature-in-Africa reproduced by skilled photogravure processes in Holland or Switzerland.

Nyiko has appeared early in the doorway. Her tender curls

sift sunlight, one pink-soled foot hooks round a tiny black ankle as she waits for her friend Gina. The little girls smile and don't speak before the others; their friendship is too deep and secret for that.

The two boys squeeze the scrapings of the mealie-meal pot into dirty balls and bait the hooks they make out of ends of wire scavenged or stolen from the broken diamond-mesh, itself scavenged, that wraps someone's fowl-cage. They murmur in the harmony of their absorption. They jump up to ask July, who is re-stacking the sheaves of thatching grass their father threw aside, if he has (ah please man July) some string? He goes away and brings a length of real plastic fishing-line bobbing a spiral from his hand. Over there, where the three stand together, Royce does (still) his little boy's dance of excitement; and Victor—

Victor is seen to clap his hands, sticky with mealie-*pap*, softly, gravely together and bob obeisance, receiving the gift with cupped palms.

At once the boys race back. You can count the beads of spinal vertebrae bent over their handiwork. Later, they pull their father from the hut and make him go fishing with their following troupe of children and babies. Red and yellow weaver-birds they disturb mass in shrill joy and flower briefly at the tips of tall grasses too slender for support.

On such a morning, lucky to be alive.

At about midday (from the height of the sun and the quiet of the bush—her watch was broken) Maureen Smales, who is alone at the hut although not alone in the settlement, no one was ever alone there—feels some change in the fabric of subconsciously identified sounds and movements that make the silence. There is a distant chuddering as of air being packed in waves of resistance against its own density. Up in the sky, yes. She is sewing the burst seam on one of her sons' shorts, good, hard-wearing stuff from Woolworths, they were never

157 ◇

got up in smart American-style leisure clothes bought for the sons of wealthy whites, or the bourgeois outfits of miniature gentlemen the poor blacks wasted money on.

The sound is not the fairly familiar one of a troop-carrier or reconnaissance plane passing. She sticks the needle like a brooch through the pants and stands to gaze. The usual cloud, lying early in wait in the west to bring rain in the afternoon, has drawn a blind over the morning, fuming with suffused sun. The chuddering grows behind it, her eyes try to follow her ears. A racket of blows that shakes the sky circles and comes down at her head—the whole village is out, now, poised in its occupations or its idleness, cringing beneath the hoverer, there is even some sort of cheer, probably from children. A high ringing is produced in her ears, her body in its rib-cage is thudded with deafening vibration, invaded by a force pumping, jigging in its monstrous orgasm—the helicopter has sprung through the hot brilliant cloud just above them all, its landing gear like spread legs, battling the air with whirling scythes.

They shriek, all of them; a woman races past Maureen laughing in terror, the baby on her back rocked amok. The whoop of their voices curves; the thrilling and terrifying thing has at once ducked up out of sight again, raising itself into the cloud. Under its belly, under the beating wings of its noise, she must have screwed up her eyes: she could not have said what colour it was, what markings it had, whether it holds saviours or murderers; and—even if she were to have identified the markings—for whom.

July's people run all around her. The dropsical one, shuffled from his stool, balanced on the two pillars of his useless legs, is holding his knob-kerrie against the sky in a warrior's homage or defiance. Martha's stance, one hand challenging dourly on her hip, is recognizable in the crowd. They are exhilarated rather than frightened; they have seen aircraft before, but never so close—the fright was more stirringly entertaining than the voice of the amplifier.

Above yells, exclamations, discussions and laughter, she follows the scudding of the engine up there behind cloud. She is following now with a sense made up of all senses. She sees the helicopter once again, a tiny dervish dangling out of cover towards the bush. It lifts once more into cloud, makes another circle of sound-waves out of sight. And then its rutting racket changes level; slows; putters.

She did not see it land, but she knows where it is. Nothing is different in the look of the bush, it is as always when her gaze flows with it, retreating before its own horizon. But she knows what it has taken in; in what direction and area the shuddering of the air has died away.

She has folded the half-sewn shorts carefully, the habit of respecting the tidiness of cupboards, and hesitating when she enters the hut, places them on the bed. Apparently not satisfied with the shorts' appearance, her palm smooths them in a forgotten caress. Then she stands for a moment while fear climbs her hand-over-hand to throttle, hold her.

She walks out of the hut. The pace quickens, stalks past the stack of thatch and the wattle fowl-cage, jolts down the incline, leaps stones, breaks into another rhythm. She is running through the elephant grass, dodging the slaps of branches, stooping through thickets of thorn. She is running to the river and she hears them, the man's voice and the voices of children speaking English somewhere to the left. But she makes straight for the ford, and pulling off her shoes balances and jumps from boulder to boulder, and when there are no more boulders does as she has seen done, moves out into the water like some member of a baptismal sect to be born again, and when the water rises to her waist, holds her arms (the shoes in one hand) high for balance while her thighs push swags of water before them. The water is tepid and brown and smells strongly of earth. It seems tilted; the sense of gravity has wavered. She is righted, suddenly come through onto the shallows of the other side and has clambered the cage of roots let down into the mud by the huge fig-tree, landmark of the bank she has never crossed to before. Her wet feet work into the shoes and she runs. A hump-backed scrub cow blunders away from the path she made for herself as she blundered upon it. She runs. She can hear the laboured muttering putter very clearly in the attentive silence of the bush around and ahead: the engine not switched off but idling, there. The real fantasies of the bush delude more inventively than the romantic forests of Grimm and Disney. The smell of boiled potatoes (from a vine indistinguishable to her from others) promises a kitchen, a house just the other side of the next tree. There are patches where airy knob-thorn trees stand free of undergrowth and the grass and orderly clumps of Barberton daisies and drifts of nemesia belong to the artful nature of a public park. She runs: trusting herself with all the suppressed trust of a lifetime, alert, like a solitary animal at the season when animals neither seek a mate nor take care of young, existing only for their lone survival, the enemy of all that would make claims of responsibility. She can still hear the beat, beyond those trees and those, and she runs towards it. She runs.